FAIRY TALE

BY

ALICE THOMAS ELLIS

FAIRY TALE

Alice Thomas Ellis

A COMMON READER EDITION
THE AKADINE PRESS

Fairy Tale

A COMMON READER EDITION published 1998
by The Akadine Press, Inc., by arrangement with the author.

A COMMON READER EDITION and fountain colophon are trademarks of
The Akadine Press, Inc.

ISBN 1-888173-40-8

1   3   5   7   9   10   8   6   4   2

FAIRY TALE

PART ONE

The eyes of the watchers were cold and flat and incurious and the watchers were still. Whenever they moved – be it ever so slightly – there was a brief darkness, a shadow behind the leaves, a hint of something that humanity might call loss, equate with pain. But the watchers knew nothing of that, being indifferent to such matters.

Eloise was sewing, sitting under the house wall, tacking lace to linen while the cat lay beside her, its stomach turned to the sun. She thought that they probably made a pretty picture and it was a pity, in a way, that there was no one to see, but few people passed by. Besides, she knew that those who might would not be touched by the scene. The shepherd, the gamekeeper would not be at all moved at the sight of her, sitting under the drooping roses. It would need a city dweller, a person of tutored observation to appreciate the contrast of white linen with her dark, voluminous dress and her long black hair, the furred, fluid lines of cat curved so trustingly at her bare feet. It was something of a waste. Simon would not catch his breath to see her. He was used to her. 'I suppose this,' said Eloise, 'is boredom.' She would not have admitted it in the presence of anyone save the cat. She began to consider further the man – it would perhaps be more interesting if it was a man – who might come walking over the hills and halt when she came into view. He would, she thought, have to be artistic, because otherwise there would be no point. Moonbird, she was sure, would agree with her. Moonbird believed in Woman's mission to share in the ongoing creative process, and after a while then, men – so she held – would see the purpose of it all. So far Simon had shown no real signs of falling into line with this development, but there was plenty of time.

Now it was getting too hot to sit outside: a drop of sweat was trickling down the side of her nose and she was wearying of her girlish fantasies: there seemed to be no possibility of their fulfilment. 'What I really want,' she said aloud, 'is a baby.' The breeze sighed as though with satisfaction, drifting indolently down the valley, soothing the grasses with an accomplished, deft finality, lifting her black hair.

The cat leapt up, its fur on end, its tail wide and its eyes furious with fear. Eloise started, staring round to see what the cat had seen. 'You are a stupid animal, M'sieu,' she told it. 'You are no proper company for me.' She was beginning to long for company.

The little red house was cool inside and smelled of woodsmoke and some old indefinable scent of its own, faint and elusive. She opened a tin of sardines and put one on a saucer for the cat, who had jumped on the back of the armchair and was gazing at the doorway. Its fur had settled but it still clearly had its reservations about something out there in the immensity of all the hills, the woods, something inimical to cats. A stoat, thought Eloise, or a vixen looking for something to quiet its cubs. It could not be the desired lone walker who had frightened the cat, for cats did not react so to humankind.

On an impulse Eloise closed the door. Perhaps it would not be good if a man came walking. She felt the hair bristle on the back of her neck. Women could be frightened as well as cats, though usually by other things. A woman then, she thought. A woman should walk past. A wise woman who would praise her sewing and tell her that in all her life she had never eaten pastry – and she had eaten a lot – as light and delicious as the pastry that Eloise laid over the apples, fragrant and sweet with cinnamon and syrup. A woman who would say, 'But of course you must have a baby. You are slender and light but your hips are wide enough, and it will be such company for you when I have gone.' For Eloise would not want her to stay too long: rather to come and go. To be wise and encouraging for a short while and then gone. She could always return if she was needed. Perhaps Moonbird might come, but Moonbird had so many calls on her time. She travelled about, dancing and lecturing, and everywhere she went women gathered round her. No one could expect Moonbird's undivided attention, for she belonged, as she often remarked, to the World.

Eloise cut half a small cucumber into slices and ate them neatly, in tiny pieces, with the smallest fork in the kitchen drawer. One of her aunts had once told her mother that she liked to take Eloise out to tea because she was so dainty in her ways. 'Eat your sardine, gross animal,' she said to M'sieu, pointing imperiously at his saucer. He was now sitting in the armchair, looking hunched and faintly glum, like a cat whom some minor calamity had befallen. He gave her a brief, contemptuous glance and stayed where he was.

Eloise washed her hands at the kitchen sink and picked up the nightdress she was working on. She made nightdresses and petticoats in the old-fashioned mode and sold them to a shop in the market town – one of those exclusive little shops with a single garment and something imaginatively incongruous – a monkey's skull or an old boot – arranged in the window. Simon took the clothes in when Eloise had made a dozen. They were all finished by hand, which made them precious and gave them a hint of pathos, as though child labour had been employed: the women who wore them might feel, at once, delicate and ruthless, like some hard-hearted princess. Eloise suspected that the women who wore them would not, in all likelihood, feel any such thing but she still sewed in fantasy with each stitch, for she was, in her way, an artist and Moonbird held that you must have faith in what you did for the good of your Karma. She had always sewed – ever since her mother's best friend had given her a beginner's embroidery kit when she was very small.

The soft smell of broken grass came through the

window. It reminded Eloise that she had chosen to live in the country and should therefore avail herself of its amenities at every opportunity. Fine, sunny days were not to be lost hiding indoors from non-existent terrors. It was not sensible, nor was it attractive. Eloise was ready to despise women who clutched their hands to their hearts at an unexpected sound and avoided fields with cows in them. Liberation meant freedom from fear as well as from the disadvantages of town life. She had made up her mind to live in the country and unless she lived in it in every possible sense she would appear foolish. Not only in her own eyes, for Simon could be perceptive: not often and not very, she reassured herself, but he sometimes surprised her with a glance or a remark that suggested he understood more than he spoke of. Eloise's mother had contrived, perhaps inadvertently, to raise her to a condition where she thought of men as, in previous times, men, it was said, had thought of women: largely brainless and good for only one thing. Eloise would not have admitted this in so many words and indeed was scarcely aware that she believed it. The ebbing tide of feminism had left detritus in many shallow waters; so evident it was beyond notice. Moonbird believed in sexual activity and the energies it unleashed but was not greatly concerned with personalities.

A flock of sheep was being driven down the lane below the house. Eloise went out to watch and listen. They made two sounds, with the high cry of the lambs and the deep call of their mothers. She sat on a low wall and looked down on the heaving, cobbled mass of shorn backs. So might a woman of ancient times have sat in the sun and watched sheep go by. The shepherd waved to her and she waved back, trying not to seem to be striving after graciousness. She wondered if he lived alone or whether he had a wife and baby. He was very large and not handsome but he looked up at her before he called to his dog. Eloise did not much care for the dog. It had an air both craven and threatening, sneaking and writhing; low to the ground around the innocent sheep, a subservient eye on its master. The attitude of the overseer. To and fro it went. Eloise was surprised at her reaction: she usually approved of dogs, being generally respectful of animals and their rights. It occurred to her that the sheep might be going to the slaughter and she stopped waving. It was wrong that animals should be trained to betray each other. It was the fault of man. Eloise yawned. Perhaps she was getting depressed, alone so much with no one to talk to. Depression was more respectable than boredom. Boredom led you into trouble while depression caused people to worry about you. When Simon came home she'd telephone her mother.

In the late afternoon Simon came up the path from the lane with his shirt knotted round his waist. His shoulders were pinkly scorched, for his skin was fair. Now people warned each other about the sun as previous generations had warned each other as to the perils inherent in getting their feet wet or their chests chilled. Sun blockers and shady hats had taken the place of galoshes and vests as the human race strove to survive, if not for ever, then for as long as it possibly could. He called, 'I'm home,' when he drew near the door. Eloise said, 'You mustn't sit in the sun like that.' Man had spoiled their relationship to the benevolent sun, making holes in the ozone layer, and it was understandably vengeful. Moonbird had contrived a placatory rite to remedy the situation but it would be some time before it took effect.

Simon said, 'I wasn't sitting in it. I was putting in fence posts.' He was a literally minded boy.

Eloise said, 'You should keep your shirt on all the same.' She thought, for just one moment, of the stranger who would be too artistic to let his skin peel or go pink in the sun and then put him out of her mind. She had made macaroni cheese for Simon's supper, and a tomato salad with mint fresh from the garden. It was quite a big garden in Eloise's opinion, and pretty. It lay behind the house, for in front there was only a narrow, paved terrace and the low wall before the ground sloped down to the lane. Simon had cleared all the weeds, the nettles and thistles and dock, and together they had planted cottage flowers. Blue geraniums and silken-petalled hollyhocks and smiling pansies and snow-in-summer. They had been too recently planted to be flourishing but poppies grew there and a gooseberry bush, and foxgloves had come uninvited but welcome. A wild rose linked branches with the brambles along the back fence and an old elder proffered saucers of creamy blossom in the far corner. There were two apple trees – one bearing a bundle of mistletoe and a pied wagtail's nest where a cuckoo had laid her egg in the springtime: it had a bowed, complaisant look – and a dying damson tree. Then there was a wide swathe of grass with buttercups and daisies and clover to sweeten it. Around the edges were bristling thistles and nettles that threatened to encroach on the flower beds but Simon kept them at bay – Moonbird held that no plant was a weed and the butterflies loved even the plainest of plants.

'You can have your supper in the garden,' said Eloise. 'In the shade,' she added, for under the trees were a table and a bench and an old wooden chair. She was truly blessed, Eloise told herself, lighting the three squat candles that were supposed to delight the goddess and repel insects. The sun was going down behind the hill that sheltered the house from the winds and the midges were coming out for the evening. Simon ate contentedly, hardly bothering to slap at the insects that sometimes bit him.

He often felt, like Eloise, that they had done the right thing in fleeing the city. They sat in silence as the shadows lengthened and grew deeper, too young to think about such boring things as compatibility.

Eloise woke in the night. There was a bird calling from somewhere. It didn't sound like an owl, but owls made unexpected noises when they forgot their words. Simon was sprawled over most of the bed. He was lying on his back, but he wasn't snoring so she couldn't hold him responsible for her wakefulness. She went to the window and knelt down to look out over the valley. It was strange how things looked different in the night. People said, 'Things will look different in the morning.' They said it when they were tired of listening and wanted to go to sleep. They said it to people who were boring them. But they were wrong. Everything looked the same every morning: all in order and just the same. It was in the nights that the difference held sway and there was no comfort for lost and lonely things. There was no one to be seen in the moonlight and nothing moved, yet Eloise knew that somewhere in the far shadow something was crying for its mother. A tear dried on her face before she crept back into bed.

'Eloise rang this morning,' said Eloise's mother. She had a three-bedroomed flat in a mansion block, and very nice too.

'What did she want?' asked Miriam, leaning back in the white-tweeded arms of a prim yet elegant chair.

'She didn't say,' said Clare. 'Or if she did I didn't get it.' She squinted into an ice-cold glass of vodka and tonic. Miriam was her oldest friend and familiar with Eloise's oddities of speech and demeanour. As a daughter Eloise was not altogether all that Clare could have wished and in the end she had admitted as much, though only of course to Miriam. It was no one else's business. At first they had attributed Eloise's ways to originality of approach: her convoluted thought processes might have been an early indication of genius, her unstudied remarks a sign of rare intelligence. As time passed, however, they had only begun to hope, albeit tacitly, that Eloise was not actually deranged. Even her passion for sewing, which had seemed so charming in a child, had begun to cause them unease, for few of her contemporaries were ever found so engaged, head down, stitching away into the night. It had been odd when it became clear that she had no interest whatsoever in exams and not the remotest intention of working for them. And it had been passing odd when, a year later, at the age of seventeen, she had persuaded a perfectly ordinary, nice boy with a promising career in advertising ahead of him to throw it all up and follow her down to a dreary little house under a hill in the depths of Wales and do woodwork.

'Woodwork,' said Clare aloud as she considered the matter. 'Wales.'

'It was very wrong of Max,' said Miriam, 'to give her all that money.'

'Exactly,' said Clare, relieved as always to shift the blame on to her ex-husband.

'On the other hand,' said Miriam, 'if he hadn't she might still be here driving you crazy.'

'I daresay I could have coped,' said Clare, torn between thwarted martyrdom and the knowledge that Miriam was right. 'I don't think I was cut out for motherhood really.' She spoke partly in deference to

12

Miriam's childless state, although Miriam had never, by word or deed, shown any hint of maternal yearnings. Miriam sipped from her glass to conceal the involuntary expression of doubt which she could feel was about to alter her face.

'She's OK, though?' she said. 'There's nothing wrong?'

'Not as far as I could tell,' said Clare. 'Nothing out of the usual. You know what she's like.' She sighed heavily in the expectation of reassurance, no matter how insincere.

'Well, at least she's out of the clutches of Bat-ears or whatever she calls herself,' said Miriam.

'Moonbird,' said Clare.

'*Moonbird*,' said Miriam. 'She was born a Weinberg or my name's Schleswig-Holstein.'

'How do you know?' asked Clare.

'I know the family,' said Miriam. 'Maybe I should wish them long life. *Moonhead*.' She wrinkled her nose.

'Moonbird,' said Clare automatically.

Eloise sang to herself – a lullaby with reference to the winds of the western sea – stopped and looked over her shoulder at the sudden stirring in the leaves. There was a breeze again today, a skittish, childlike breeze that lifted her hair. She'd been washing old lace, bought from the market, and she was putting it to dry on the wall, scoured clean by ages of rain and wind; carefully choosing immaculate pebbles to weight it down.

Meadowsweet and Queen Anne's lace grew among the nettles in the lane – lovelier than hers no doubt, but not so resilient. She looked behind her again but no one was there. No more than she'd expected. When she turned and looked below there were four men walking up the lane, trying to avoid the ruts and hollows by treading the grass in the middle. They looked extraordinary in the morning sunlight, for they wore city suits and shirts and ties, they carried briefcases and their shoes gleamed blindingly. For a moment Eloise thought she'd never seen anything so incongruous and she wondered whether it might be wise to go into the house and slam the door. Shut out the intruders. But she stood still, her hands at her sides, and she remembered how, yesterday, she had longed for company.

'Good morning,' they said as they came closer. All of them. They spoke together, though on different notes. 'Good morning, good morning . . .'

'Good morning,' said Eloise. They sounded like the sheep, she thought. Making noises in their various ways. The leader opened the gate and they came up the path to where she stood and they stood around her, smiling.

'So of course,' said Eloise, 'I thought they were Jehovah's Witnesses or Mormons or something.'

'They go round in pairs,' said Simon.

'Yes, I know that,' said Eloise. 'But there might have been two pairs of them.'

'Well, get on with it,' said Simon. 'What did they want?'

'I'm not sure,' said Eloise, 'but I think they wanted to buy the place.'

'Jehovah's Witnesses?' said Simon. 'They don't want to buy places. They want to sell you the *Watchtower*.'

'How do you know that?' asked Eloise.

'Everyone knows that,' said Simon, scratching his hairline. 'They get everywhere, like the midges.'

'Well, they weren't Jehovah's Witnesses,' Eloise assured him. 'I asked.'

'So what were they? Insurance salesmen, civil servants, social workers?'

'No,' said Eloise. 'They said they were the Order of something and I asked if they were Christians and they just looked at each other and then they looked at me. They were very friendly.' She wished now that she had listened more carefully to what they had said. Her mind had wandered as they stood there talking, but she didn't want Simon to know that. Young as he was, he had already developed masculine views on the reliability of the female mind.

'I don't like the sound of them,' he said, suddenly the man of the house, the householder. 'I don't like you being here on your own,' added this person who had not before expressed anxiety for her in her solitariness. 'If they come back I'll have a word with the police.' The police, as far as Eloise was aware, consisted of a man and a boy and a white vehicle in the third village away.

15

The larger force was mostly kept busy by the disaffected youth in the market town who had nothing to do. Interested parties had formed a Farm Watch organization since a certain amount of sheep rustling went on and a number of outlying barns had been denuded of the slates on their roofs, but as far as she knew there was little violence among the rural population except on a purely domestic level. 'Since they built the motorways,' said Simon, 'criminals can come from the cities down to the country, steal what they like, and be back in the city in no time.'

'We haven't got anything to steal,' said Eloise.

'How would they know?' demanded Simon. 'You might have the family jewels hidden under the floorboards. They'll take anything these days – to buy drugs,' he added. Simon came of a generation of middle-class youth which eschewed the use of the harder drugs since they had become widely available to the lower classes, while most of the upper classes who had been gripped by addiction had been able to afford to die of it. The romance had gone. He would, if challenged, have denied that this social phenomenon was a symptom of snobbery, and claimed, rather, that he had too much sense. He didn't even drink very much.

'When I've got the shed up,' he said, 'I'll be able to work at home and you won't be alone.' He planned to build this shed and put a lathe in it, whereupon he would be able to construct small articles of carpentry and sell them. Many people now considered this a perfectly respectable occupation for a boy of the middle class. In the meantime he hired himself out to anyone who wanted a hand doing almost anything on the farms and estates around, although he drew the line at dealing with livestock. He also enjoyed travelling about in his van and meeting people, but this was never mentioned. It would have been disconcerting for Eloise who, as Simon imagined, was too rare to crave for company.

'If I had a baby,' said Eloise, who was beginning to say this rather often, 'I wouldn't be lonely.'

'A baby would be no protection,' said Simon, taken aback at this unexpected admission of weakness.

'I don't want protection,' said Eloise. 'I want company.' Simon was startled afresh.

'Then ask your mother to stay,' he said. There was a short, uneasy silence. They had, so far, never quarrelled because, since they had chosen to live together against the fervent advice of families and friends, dissent between them would have been evidence of failure. Anyone could have come along and said, 'I told you so.' There had been no need to discuss this: it lay between them forming their strongest bond – or shackle, depending on how you looked at it.

'You're too young to have a baby,' said Simon. 'You've got all your life ahead of you.'

Eloise, who was peeling potatoes at the sink, remained silent although she let the knife slip from her hand into the cold water, leaving the last potato intact. 'You ...' he had said, and 'You ...', as though he thought only of her and cared nothing for her. Any adviser to any supplicant, whose best interests were his main concern. Showing her the way to freedom when all she wanted was to stay where she was – only not alone.

'Don't you love me?' she asked. She expected Simon to love her. It was only right and proper that he should love her more than she loved him. He had her as reward for his devotion and she saw no need for exaggerated reciprocity. What more could he want?

'Of course I love you,' said Simon crossly. How could she doubt it? 'Only we don't want a baby yet.'

'I do,' said Eloise, resenting the plural. 'I want a baby more than anything else in the world.'

Simon wanted to shout. He wanted to scream – you can't have one. The prospect of a baby filled him with misery. He knew about babies and Eloise did not. It was debatable whether she'd ever seen one close up, for her family did not go in much for babies – not as his did. When he was thirteen his mother had given birth to his sister, thereby, he considered, greatly hindering his development into manhood. Just as he was easing his way into the adult world that world had changed, had regressed from being a place fragrant with cigar and brandy fumes, a place where doors opened on to sophisticated sights and cool jokes were exchanged, into a terrible pastel paleness full of the smell of anxiety and milk and nappies, and sticky with smears of half-chewed biscuit and banana. Things had ceased to be amusing.

Simon had determined, as he entered adolescence, never to be a family man. He had somehow failed to take into account the fact that if you ran away with a girl and set up house with her, you had trodden the first step on the path to that awful destiny. Fleeing his own family in the quest for love and gaiety and freedom, he now appeared to have walked, smack, into the trap. One day, naturally, he had intended to have children, but not yet. Only when he was much older and had a club to retire to. He had not defined this image with any great precision but it had been his goal nonetheless. Rather like the hope of peaceful death: accepting the inevitable but not being so unwary as to rush upon it.

'It won't be any trouble,' said Eloise. 'It can lie in its cradle while I sew and I'll feed it when it's hungry. Millions of people have babies.' She was growing more determined in the face of his opposition.

'Oh, Eloise,' said Simon, remembering the trouble his sister had caused him. The emotion and the time his mother had expended on the baby. The way her concentration had been deflected from all else. 'If only you knew.'

'Knew what?' demanded Eloise. 'Knew what?' She carried the cat up to bed that night and when she went to sleep it lay on Simon's feet until he got cramp. He didn't try to dislodge it because he loved it, but lay awake listening to the owls as they hunted and wondering why he felt lonely.

*

'So this morning Simon rang,' said Clare. 'Come into the kitchen while I tell you.' Obediently Miriam got to her feet, gathering up the vodka bottle. 'He says Eloise is missing me.'

'Does he?' said Miriam, interested.

'That's what I thought,' said Clare, who seldom failed to get the gist of even her friend's briefest remarks. 'Well, that'll be a first, I thought.' Eloise had never, in her young life, given much indication of umbilical attachment, of filial devotion. 'Where, I asked myself, is the catch in this one?'

'And where was it?' inquired Miriam.

'He didn't say,' said Clare. 'I probed a bit, danced round the question, gave him a few openings but he didn't say.'

'What did he sound like?' asked Miriam. Clare shrugged.

'Like they always sound,' she said. 'They all sound the same.' She was speaking of the young. 'They never really tell you anything so then you wonder whether there's really anything to tell.'

'Sometimes there is,' said Miriam. Clare agreed morosely. She had been shaken when Eloise had declared her intention of going to live in the country and make nightdresses. Her ex-husband had stated categorically that it was all her fault and in the future he was going to make himself responsible for his daughter's welfare. He hadn't, of course, except for giving her money.

'They wouldn't think of ringing her father, naturally,' she said.

'So they can't be short of money,' mused Miriam aloud.

'Not unless they've been lighting fires with it,' said Clare, who was constantly slightly resentful of the paucity of her alimony. She had never felt the need of a career and had married in the expectation of wealth and lifelong security.

'And what does Simon expect you to do?' asked Miriam, topping up her vodka glass.

'I think he wants me to go and stay,' said Clare. 'Why else would he tell me that Eloise is lonely?'

'Few men,' said Miriam, 'want their mother-in-law to come and stay. It isn't in nature. Are you sure that's what he said?'

'No,' said Clare, 'I'm not, but I can't think what else he wanted. And I'm not your usual mother-in-law,' she added, with a distasteful picture in her mind of a woman with plastic shoes and handbag. 'I'm not a mother-in-law at all if we're going to be accurate.'

'Then there must be a crisis,' said Miriam. 'When are you going?' There was a short hesitation before Clare spoke. Miriam, although, or perhaps because, she was not married and had no children, held strong opinions about familial duty and responsibility.

'I can't go,' she said. 'Not just now. And don't ask me why.'

'Why?' asked Miriam inevitably, as people will. She

hadn't wanted to ask but she found she couldn't help it. Clare ignored her and spread some smoked salmon on a plate. She was not, at the moment, ready to explain to her friend that she was waiting for a telephone call from a man she had met at dinner. It was too early, too speculative and she did not wish to appear eager or enthusiastic.

'It can't be a crisis,' she said. 'If it was a crisis he'd have told me, wouldn't he?'

'Crises vary,' said Miriam. 'If she hasn't broken her leg she may be depressed.'

'I can't see why not breaking a leg should depress her,' said Clare gaily. Miriam frowned.

'Don't be clever, dear. It doesn't go with your hair.' Clare had had her hair cut short like a little boy's. 'You're trying to evade the issue.'

'No I'm not,' said Clare, who was relieved that she had evaded the question of why it was so imperative that she should not leave town. 'She's grown up, after all. I can't go rushing off after her every time she calls.'

'She didn't call,' Miriam reminded her. 'Simon did.'

'Well, there you are then,' said Clare obscurely.

Over their meagre though stylish supper they discussed other matters: old love affairs, old betrayals; all the vicissitudes that afflict the living; with special attention to how these had affected their friends, and passing reference to the disturbance they had caused in high places: the government, the throne, the film, newspaper and cosmetic industries. When they had, to their own satisfaction, understood the hidden and convoluted psychological complexities that lay behind these events, Clare felt the need to revert to the more interesting and immediate topic of herself. She had drunk most of the wine, since Miriam was of a more abstemious disposition, and was now in the mood for confidences. She approached the subject, as she thought, obliquely.

'So who is he?' demanded Miriam. 'Who is this Claud? You've mentioned his name twenty-five times in the past five minutes. Explain this to me.'

'He's a television producer,' said Clare, caught on the hop.

'I see,' said Miriam. She looked a bit like a lion when she smiled, thought Clare, who was under the impression that she had been describing a dinner party in general terms preparatory to introducing the subject of Claud.

'You're hopeless,' said Miriam. She had been waiting for Clare to fall for a Chinese so she could remark, 'Out of the frying pan into the wok,' but had not yet had the chance. She mentioned this, saying that her hopes had been raised last week in a restaurant in Gerrard Street but that she had been disappointed.

'Claud's French,' said Clare, ignoring the imputation that she flirted with waiters.

'They don't like us,' said Miriam. 'We don't match up to their ideal of womanhood.'

'Rubbish,' said Clare inadequately.

'We dribble,' said Miriam, wiping a trickle of melon

juice from her chin. 'If a Frenchman knew you refused to go and tend your ailing daughter he would be profoundly disgusted. He'd go straight and tell his *maman*. She'd be disgusted too. Or am I thinking of Italians?'

'You're thinking Jewish,' said Clare. 'You think I'm cold and unfeeling.'

'So you are,' said Miriam. 'I'm ashamed of you.'

'Then why don't *you* go?' demanded Clare. 'You're her godmother.' This was obviously not strictly so, but Miriam knew what was meant. From the moment of Eloise's birth she had accepted, had been compelled to accept, a degree of responsibility for her best friend's child. If your best friend was something of a *nebbish* what else could you do? She had been present at the birth. Eloise had arrived unexpectedly in the bathroom after Clare had made an unsuitable choice of luncheon dish. Either that or she had got her dates wrong.

'I haven't been asked,' said Miriam.

'You don't need to be asked,' said Clare, seeing through this feeble excuse. 'You need a holiday. You keep saying so.' Miriam had become involved in good works. These were not, in themselves, too onerous, but the people you got to mix with . . . Miriam had frequently spoken of them. 'All those committees,' Clare continued. 'All those meetings, all that paperwork, the *people* . . .'

'All right, all right,' said Miriam.

'And it'll be lovely down there now,' said Clare. 'All the flowers will be out, and the birds . . .'

'I'm not what you could call a bird-lover,' said Miriam. 'I don't see the point of them.'

'Don't interrupt,' Clare rebuked her, seizing the advantage. Not having been met with a blank negative she grew enthusiastic. 'You'll have perfect peace, nothing to do all day, a real, wonderful rest.' Observing that Miriam's expression could be described as sardonic, she paused in the expectation of some caustic response. Miriam said nothing but tapped the table top rhythmically with two fingers. 'I mean it,' said Clare. 'You won't just be doing me a favour, you'll have a nice time.' Seen from this distance the countryside did indeed seem appealing. From the balcony of her mansion block she could look down on the traffic and the crowds of tourists searching vainly in the streets and squares for the qualities that made the city unique, different from anywhere else. They had mostly already visited the Tower of London, Camden Lock with its world-famed shop called Chain Reaction where you could buy a present for anyone, Fortnum & Mason's, and seen the Changing of the Guard. Under the hand of planners and architects and the proliferation of franchises the city was growing daily indistinguishable from everywhere else in the world. And when you went out in those streets you wished you hadn't. 'No crowds, no cars, no noise, no filth,' said Clare, her tone strengthening with conviction.

'No theatres, no museums, no restaurants, no bars, no clubs,' said Miriam.

'Peace,' insisted Clare. 'Perfect peace.' She felt, under

the circumstances, that she could permit herself a little hyperbole.

Again Eloise sat in the garden, sewing, but she worked listlessly, without concentration, and so, as is always the case when authority fails, her members became un-controlled and the fingers of her left hand ran the needle cruelly into the first finger of her right. 'Damn,' said Eloise as a drop of blood stained the snowy whiteness of the nightdress. 'Now look what you made me do,' she said to the cat, who was sitting blamelessly in an ar-rangement of buttercups. Even if it understood her it was too realistic to take any notice of this injustice.

When the four men appeared at the gate Eloise felt no apprehension but a sudden renewed vitality. 'Come in,' she invited them. 'I'll make some coffee.' Her invitation was unnecessary, for they were already coming, in single file, up the narrow, slate-flagged path. They were led by the smallest of them: a man whose smile reminded her of a rowing boat, seen from above. Behind came a large man, and in the rear came two who to Eloise's eyes were indistinguishable, each from the other. They stood around her, declining the offer of coffee, and each looked about him in a different direction – to the north and the south and the east and the west.

'Nice place you've got here,' said the small one. Eloise was disappointed at the banality of this remark. She had expected something more original.

'What Order do you belong to?' she asked, outright.

They did not answer. They might not have heard her for all the notice they took of her question.

'Did you ever think of selling?' asked the large one and she felt quite let down. They were after all mere estate agents: a breed which Eloise had learned to hold in contempt.

'Never,' she said coldly. Once, and had they been of a different sort, she would have explained that this place was the fulfilment of her heart's desire and she would never leave until she was carried out, feet first. She was no longer as convinced of this as she had been but nothing would persuade her to confess it. Not to anyone.

The four altered their demeanour; a message seemed to pass between them and they acted in concert. They said variously that the day was hot, the way up the lane was long, that they were a little thirsty, and that it would be good to sit down ... Eloise was reassured as they said these everyday things. She brought out a pitcher of water and four glasses, all matching, while the big man and the twins sat on the wall and the little one stood, admiring the view. He admired all of it, turning to the back and the front and the sides of it. The big man watched him, his eyes unblinking, and Eloise had a fleeting impression that it was he who was in charge here, was the leader, not the small spokesman who was made to go first. 'A very nice place,' he said in a deep voice, suitable to his size.

Eloise went back into the house to refill the pitcher. Looking through the window she saw them, heads together, talking earnestly, and wondered what they had to discuss. As she came out they parted, three of them sitting up straight and the little one standing squarely and gazing at her. 'We are going to leave some literature for your perusal,' he said.

'I'm not . . .' began Eloise.

'No, no,' he said. 'You can keep your house. We want you to read this very carefully. Remember we're thinking about you. We think a lot of you.' Eloise found this speech so remarkable that she could summon up nothing to say. 'Thank you' seemed inappropriate, for who was he to permit her to keep her house? And why should they think of her? And did they expect her to be grateful for what was, when you came to consider it, impertinence from a stranger? She was astonished and had no room for anger. As they left, their shoes shining in the morning sun, she thought they looked more incongruous than if they had been clad in Roman armour, plumes waving from their helmeted heads above the wall. The whiteness of their shirts put to shame the sullied nightgown with its splash of scarlet. She wondered who did their washing. The leaflets she barely glanced at but she put them in the kitchen drawer, not at the back of the fireplace. Later she found she could hardly remember their words – as though they had spoken in a half-known language about some trivial topic. Like a conversation about the weather in a foreign bar.

She looked round for the cat: it wasn't in any of its usual places. It was not in the house and not in the garden. 'Cat,' she called, 'Ca-a-a-a-t, M'sieu, M'sieu,' and her voice echoed under the hill and across the valley. She stopped when she heard herself shouting. It was strange that the sound of your own voice could alarm you, but as the silence settled it seemed to hold a hint of reproach. Eloise was cowed and glad there was no one to hear or to see her. The watchers were still.

M'sieu came back as evening fell. He came with Simon, purring round his sturdy ankles. He had never done that before, but it seemed of no significance, so neither of them remarked on it. He was a young cat and would doubtless develop other habits in the course of his nine lives.

'How was your day?' they asked each other as Eloise scrubbed potatoes and washed herbs for a salad. She had persuaded Simon to share her vegetarian diet. It was easy for the person who did the cooking to impose her will on others.

For a time Simon had bought meat from the butcher in the far village, but Eloise had told him that if he wished to eat it he would have to cook it himself. She had fled disgustedly into the garden, away from the sacrificial smell of burning fat, and in the end he had found it less wearisome to eat what was put before him. It was simple enough, when he was passing one of the few shops in the district, to buy meat pies and boiled ham and eat them far away from Eloise's disapproving gaze.

She had thought of converting M'sieu to a high-protein, meatless diet, but he wouldn't eat beans and chickpeas so she had compromised by feeding him only fish. It was not right but it was less wrong than permitting him to devour other mammals. So far he had not defied her by bringing in mice or birds. Moonbird said that as the human race progressed towards perfection under the outspread skirts of Goddess, then the beasts, who had learned most of their bad, violent habits from the example of men, would also improve significantly.

'I baled hay,' said Simon, the evidence on him as a few stalks of golden grass fell to the floor.

'The men came back,' said Eloise, tossing the salad. Her tone held both pathos and a little pride. Simon had known boys who used that tone when they had been slightly but honourably injured on the sports field. He found it annoying since it had usually turned out to be their own fault when you came to look at it dispassionately.

'Why did you let them in?' he inquired. Eloise was irked at the lack of sympathy. She had been expecting a repeat of his earlier response, a manly insistence on informing the police, whereupon she could have dismissed his fears, saying that the men were obviously harmless and implying that they had enjoyed her company.

'I didn't let them in,' she said. 'They sat in the garden and I gave them water.' She slapped his salad down on a plate in front of him and banged down a baked potato, like an infliction, beside it. 'They were very interested to see that I'm left-handed,' she added. 'They could hardly take their eyes off my sewing.'

'Don't sulk,' said Simon, resigned to a supper of tubers and leaves. 'I worry about you, that's all.'

'I don't suppose they'd murder me,' comforted Eloise, who was sufficiently good-natured when her selfishness was satisfied.

'I don't suppose they'd mean to,' said Simon, his mouth full of a grass-like substance, 'but if they were looking for antiques and you got in the way they might. It isn't like the old days,' he went on, having been told this by almost everyone he met almost every day. 'There are some very nasty types about who'll stick at nothing.' He also read the newspaper during his lunch break when there was one lying around. There was no newsagent within reasonable distance but the other men brought tabloids for the racing and Simon read the pages that dwelt, in their uninformed but enthusiastic fashion, on human iniquity.

'They don't want antiques,' explained Eloise rather uncertainly, reluctant to admit that she didn't really know. 'They want the house. They said so. They said did I want to sell.'

'So what did you say?' demanded Simon, laying down his knife and fork, as though he suspected she might have sold it over his head.

'I said they couldn't have it,' said Eloise, 'and they went away.' She didn't mention the leaflets, partly because they seemed unimportant, but partly because she was young and foolish enough to savour a secret.

'They've been twice now,' said Simon. 'They could be

Nationalists if they want the house. They might resent incomers. I'll ask if anyone in the village knows anything about them, and if they come again I'll do something about it.' Eloise didn't ask what. She was old enough to recognize rhetoric when she heard it and she didn't want to hurt Simon's feelings with sensible questions. 'They might burn the place down if they can't buy it,' said Simon unguardedly. 'But I don't suppose they will,' he added, not wanting apprehension to cloud their idyll too darkly.

After a while Eloise gave M'sieu another sardine, hopefully putting a bit of potato beside it. 'He's been acting very peculiarly,' she told Simon. 'He ran away and didn't come back for hours and hours.'

'He was waiting for me by the gate,' said Simon almost smugly.

'He wasn't there all the time,' said Eloise. 'He must have been up the hill and in the woods.' Simon looked concerned. Cats were the only animals he liked, and of them all he liked this one best.

'He shouldn't do that,' he said. 'You never know what's lurking up there.'

He sounded to Eloise more worried about the cat and its wanderings than he had been about her and her visitors, but she didn't really mind. She was sure that if the Nationalists burned down the red house then Simon would rescue her before he sought the cat. M'sieu was now the very picture of a cheerful animal, eating sardine, eschewing potato. He had a short memory and had cast from his mind whatever it was he had found disturbing.

'Perhaps he was frightened of the shepherd's dog,' said Eloise.

Clare was pretending to herself that she was tidying up the sitting-room, gathering together newspapers and magazines with special attention to the area round the telephone. It had mocked her twice this morning, ringing urgently and then speaking with voices in which she had no interest. Since she paid its bills it should surely show some consideration for her wishes. She held an anthropomorphic attitude to machines, suspecting them all of a primitive but deliberate malignity. When it rang again she jumped, despite her expectations, but it was only Miriam asking her out to lunch. As she protested that she was too busy Miriam over-rode her excuses, saying that it was a lovely day and the walk to the restaurant would do her good. In Miriam's opinion Clare took insufficient exercise. Useless for Clare to imply that a large luncheon would militate against the beneficial consequences of a walk. Miriam said briskly that she could eat salad and told her to be there at one o'clock.

Emerging from the portals of her mansion block, which were still moderately imposing although no longer manned by a person in livery, Clare hailed a cab, directing it to disgorge her just before they reached the restaurant. There was no sense in openly defying Miriam.

'But just look at the prices,' she said when she was seated at a linen-clothed table opposite her friend. The prices were no more prohibitive than they had been for some time, but Clare felt she had to make a stand.

'Never mind,' said Miriam, 'I shall pay the bill,' thus subtly putting Clare back in the wrong.

'Then I shall have some asparagus to begin with,' said Clare, 'and lemon sole to follow.' She folded the menu and put it on an adjacent table. 'So, how've you been?'

'Much the same,' said Miriam. It was two days since they had last met. She leaned over the table to look closely at Clare, who attempted to shrink back and failed. It was a small, though exclusive, restaurant. 'You look peaky,' she observed.

'So do you,' said Clare, nettled. 'You look as though a long stay in the country would do you the world of good.'

'Hmm,' said Miriam, thoughtfully breaking up a bread stick.

Encouraged, Clare went on. 'Eloise would rather see you than me. You're more fun. You're not related to her. You know relations never agree about anything. They get mad at the least thing, especially with their mothers.'

'You do exaggerate,' said Miriam. 'She's nearly eighteen now. She's past the rebellious stage.'

'No she isn't,' said Clare. Not that Eloise had ever revolted in the manner of some of her contemporaries: she had simply been immovably obstinate. 'If you look back,' she continued, 'you will recall how stubborn she

was over Simon – and before that, when you think of it.'
They both remembered a certain birthday party when
Eloise had flatly refused to blow out her few candles
because she liked the light.

'I'll think about it,' said Miriam. After all, not being
Eloise's mother she had not suffered from her inexplicable intractability in the same way as had Clare. She
could see that since Eloise's flight had been so recent
there would be a certain awkwardness in the situation if
her mother arrived still in a critical frame of mind.
'Simon's a nice boy,' she said, apparently apropos of
nothing.

'I've never denied that,' said Clare, not altogether ac-
curately. She had said some rude things about Simon,
though fortunately not in his hearing. It would have
taken a long time to bring about a reconciliation if she
had openly insulted her daughter's chosen mate. 'But he
is only a boy. How can he look after her properly?'
Miriam was pleased with this evidence of maternal concern: it was clearly heart-felt and she looked away, cross-
ing her eyes a little guiltily, having imagined that Clare's
reasons for her reluctance to leave town were associated
merely with the fabulous Claud. Claud she did not mention. If Clare had not spoken his name it could mean
only one thing: Claud had not come up to scratch.

Miriam reverted to the topic of Simon. 'A nice, *manly*
boy,' she said. 'Considering the sort of people she seems
to like, he might have had ringlets down to his waist.'

'Dreadlocks,' corrected Clare knowledgeably.

35

'Or worse, gone round in a yellow frock being gentle with the baby.'

'They haven't got a baby,' Clare reminded her.

'They will have,' said Miriam. Clare looked unenthusiastic. If Eloise had a baby then she would be a grandmother.

'A little grandchild,' said Miriam meanly. Her best friend, as best friends often are, was quite transparent to her. Clare looked stricken and Miriam was contrite.

Towards the end of the week Eloise, half-stunned with ennui, put down the cloth she had been cutting up to make a petticoat and walked round the back of the house to the garden. She was amazed and hurt to find herself capable of such negative emotion. It wasn't fair. She had sacrificed all the stimulus of city life for a cleaner, clearer existence, only to discover that nothing ever happened. She had come to an ancient Celtic land to rediscover her spiritual roots, to grow close to the earth – and the sky and the moon and the stars – and nothing happened. Previously she had been scornful of happenings, parties and clubs and evenings in pubs, but now she began to realize that they did fill up the time. She had despised people with regular jobs as much as she had looked down on the unemployed, taking her own circumstances, unthreatened by penury, for granted. No one could accuse her of not working, for she made pretty night and underwear, sewing and washing and ironing it like a good girl. And she kept the house clean and looked after Simon and was kind to the cat. Unfamiliar with the concept of self-pity she gazed out, aggrieved, at a careless world, wondering mistily who she could blame. A nice little baby would make all the difference. She would line its little basket with the finest of lawn and bathe it in a little tub, outside in the sunshine. Walking round the garden she passed the gooseberry bush and paused to peer under it hopefully. There was no one to see her, and even if there were they would think she was investigating the state of the nascent gooseberries, not looking for babies. In this assumption Eloise was mistaken.

Lingering over a tedious snack of herbs and tomato she remembered the leaflets in the kitchen drawer and took them out. She washed up her plate and knife and fork and went to lie under the elder tree and read. The leaflets did not look like the sort of thing that estate agents pressed on the public. They were printed in a strange script, almost impossible to comprehend, and were copiously illustrated with childlike line drawings of leaves and berries, mushrooms, nuts and flowers. Eloise decided the men must, after all, be foreign missionaries seeking for converts. Or possibly seed salesmen, she thought, yawning, and fell asleep. When she woke it was well past tea-time and the air was growing cold, a breeze stirring the leaves above her head and the shadows creeping closer. Something that was not quite fear kept her lying still for a moment, reluctant to move lest the disturbance reveal her presence. It would not be advisable to make an alien noise or gesture in the darkening hush. The birds had fallen silent and the only sound was the paper-thin rustling of leaves. The edges of the leaflets on the ground beside her rose gently in accord with that slow, inquisitive breeze. Growing chilled, Eloise leapt to her feet, snatched up her leaflets and then, between bravado and apology, walked purposefully across what she considered was her own grass into her own house.

'I am one with nature,' she said aloud. Held in the strong, warm embrace of Goddess. And she herself a strong, warm female with nothing to fear but fear itself. Deeply in touch with the Mother she was invulnerable. Moonbird said so.

Every now and then for the briefest moment Eloise wondered whether Moonbird did not talk very great nonsense but she always thrust away these doubts, for without her beliefs there would be no purpose in life. There was something uncanny around her but it gave no sense of benevolence. It was not what she had expected. She was dimly aware of inimical appraisal where she had looked for unqualified acceptance. Somewhere in Eloise there now lay the disagreeable suspicion that she had not behaved with the circumspection proper to even a free spirit. She had not attained the degree of serenity she had anticipated and was beginning to suspect herself of a certain lack of foresight.

'I'm home,' called Simon. 'Why haven't you got the

light on?' he asked as he came through the door. Sometimes light, like water, washed away all the dark things, but sometimes it didn't. Sometimes, by contrast yet in collaboration, it served the dark things well, showing what it were better not to see . . .

'It's not dark enough yet,' said Eloise, but Simon knocked against a stool and swore mildly.

'Leave the door open,' she said from the armchair. There was something out there that she was loth to admit to her mind; should they close the door it would be an admission that there was something to admit, to let in . . . Fumbling with this thought she sat still.

'What's for supper?' asked Simon, puzzled to see her sitting so silently at such a time. Usually there was movement when he came home, the flames in the fireplace, the running of the tap, Eloise skipping from the cupboard to the sink preparing things to eat, the cat, like himself, shifting around in anticipation. Now there wasn't even a bluebottle complaining in the restless, illtempered way of its kind. A profane peace hung over the household. Simon snapped on the light switch.

'Nut cutlets and mash,' said Eloise, coming back to life.

Alone in her flat Clare still sat in the twilight; the city twilight of fumy umber with undertones of garish yellow and a far hint of crimson. The banded air lay below her windows but no stars were yet visible. Her enemy crouched on its desk, triumphantly, wickedly silent. 'Ring, you bloody thing,' said Clare, and when it refused she made herself a vodka martini, so that when Simon telephoned she was far from sober.

'Your mother says Miriam wants to come down,' said Simon in the morning, the innocent morning.

'When did she say that?' asked Eloise.

'Last night,' he said. He did not disclose who had telephoned whom and Eloise didn't ask because she didn't care. 'When you were asleep,' he added superfluously.

Eloise ruminated over her blackcurrant tea. A month ago, she would have expressed dissatisfaction with this proposal, have said that she was more than content to be alone and a visit from anyone would be an intrusion on the integrity of her solitude. Not that she would have put it quite like that. No. She would have said, rather, that Miriam was a nosy old thing, her mother's creature, sent to spy on her. It would not have occurred to her that Miriam might be weary of the city and craving the solace of the countryside. Nor did it now, correctly as it happened, but Eloise was too solipsistic to entertain the possibility that anyone connected with her might have motives or aims not directly concerned with herself. Miriam was good company despite her age – she must be as old as Clare – and not much given to covert disapproval, an attitude which drove Eloise, in common with most of the rest of mankind, nearly mad. Miriam got cross but she didn't brood about it.

'When's she coming?' she inquired abruptly. Simon was surprised, having expected protests, if not a blank refusal to permit her mother's closest friend to set foot in her garden.

'I don't know,' said Simon. 'You'd better ring and ask her.' He finished his toast and went to repair a barn door for a farmer.

It was too early to phone a city person; time was weighted differently there, sliding with heavy emphasis into evening and night. Few people got to work or even woke before dawn had shaken off the dark. Even 10 a.m. seemed early to modern town dwellers. Having made up her mind, Eloise was impatient to further her plans. She would clean the spare room and put flowers in it. She did that and looked at the clock which was idly ticking by with no sense of urgency, making no concessions to the impulsive nature of mankind. Eloise had inherited her mother's mistrust of mechanisms and eyed it with disfavour. By half past eight she could wait no longer.

Miriam answered immediately, leading Eloise to suppose that she was still in bed and had reached out a sleepy hand to the telephone which stood on her bedside table. Eloise kept hers in the tiny space at the foot of the stairs, for she considered it sybaritic and slightly vulgar to have the telephone by your bed. Many of Eloise's prejudices were rooted in an earlier age, and her mother had often wondered aloud where she got them from.

Miriam said that she would drive down in four days' time. First, she explained, she must alert her colleagues to the fact that dogsbody would not be around for a while. The thought was invigorating and her smile made her voice affectionate.

Eloise too was revivified, living now not in the present with its tiresomely material aspects and the shaming knowledge that she was uneasy in her solitude, but in the near future which she could form as she wished, forgetting that the clock would inexorably bring her visionary aspirations to reality. She foresaw the comfort of company; the shared laughter, the wine, the praise, and besides, since Miriam was coming in her car, they could go out and see other places, other scenes and have lunch in pubs. If she were threatened with a knife Eloise would not have admitted to a yearning to lunch in pubs. That was her secret. Ready prepared for utterance in the forefront of her mind, like cold dishes, were the phrases that would convince outsiders that she had made an inspired and rewarding decision in giving up everything to come and live in the country. The wild flowers were reappearing in the fields and hedgerows since pesticides were no longer used so much. That would interest Miriam.

She went into the back garden to sew before the sun got high. In her lap lay a very small garment in the early stages of manufacture. As time went by she would embroider it with white violets and it would be described by all who saw it as exquisite, for she was, it was unanimously conceded, clever with her needle. The sun rose above the hill and the shade retreated. Dazzled, she looked up and blinked, called back from a dream of infant limbs and downy heads, of milk and honey.

The men had come so silently that she was unaware of them until the small one spoke. They stood round her, beaming down benevolently like close friends, as though they had known and loved her all her life. Eloise did not respond appropriately. It was not the mindless affection of strangers that she sought, which was why she had so few friends, but the approval of the small number of people who, for whatever reason, she considered significant. It might be that Moonbird was too taken up with her mission to visit but Miriam would soon be here and she had no need of passing strangers. As the hours had gone by she had looked forward more to Miriam's imminent arrival. So what if Miriam had backed Clare in disapproving of what Eloise thought of as her elopement? So what if she had smacked her leg when she was eleven and paid for a maths tutor when she was fifteen? So what if she had openly asked Moonbird what she thought she was doing, acting like a lunatic? (Moonbird had explained that her destiny lay outside the narrow confines of family and orthodox religion and Miriam had cast her a look of scorn.) These errors of judgement were all in the past and surely due only to thoughtlessness, a failure to consider in sufficient depth the qualities and aims of her friend's daughter. She had meant well, and when she wasn't worrying about other people's behaviour she was undeniably good company. What was more, she would certainly be impressed by the nightdresses. Eloise, concentrating on Miriam's good side, was now impatient with the men who were endeavouring to waste her time. They were redundant in her garden and she applied herself to her sewing so as not to give the impression they could stand about for as long as they liked, waiting for her to bring them water. The silence drew on until she looked up to catch them consulting one another with glances and small gestures. It was as though her acknowledgement of their presence gave them liberty to speak. They sat down, the large one in the chair and the twins on the grass, which Eloise considered over-familiar: you did not sit, uninvited, on a person's grass unless you were more than just an aquaintance. It looked as though you meant to stay.

The little man stood and addressed her. 'Did you peruse the reading matter we left for you?' he inquired.

'Yes,' said Eloise shortly.

'And what did you think of it?' he continued. Eloise stared at him. Above all else she disliked being interrogated. Only Simon had the right to question her and he knew where to draw the line. She had not thought ever to encounter another examiner.

'Nothing,' she said, which was more or less the answer she had given to the queries presented by O levels.

'Then shall we run through it together?' he offered, reaching for his briefcase, not seeming greatly surprised by her response. 'There is a great deal for you to learn . . .'

'I'm very busy at the moment,' said Eloise, beginning to sew again, regretting her previous tolerance of these men. Unwanted company was worse than loneliness. She shifted huffily on the corner of the bench; perhaps if their ears did not convince them, their eyes might prove that she wanted them gone. They took no notice. The twins had their eyes on the baby's dress. She shook it irritably and glared at them, wondering why it was no longer possible to be politely rude in the legendary way of people's great-grandmothers. This was the sort of thing Eloise knew about: no one could think quite how or why. Haughty glances were now known as dirty looks. It was no longer possible to 'cut' someone in the street; they simply didn't notice, imagining that you hadn't seen them and ringing up later to ask, jovially, what you had on your mind. In order to insult a person you had to raise your voice and use swear words. All subtlety had gone from society and there was a popular consensus that people greatly cared for each other and enjoyed being together. Eloise, who was rigidly selective, found herself at a disadvantage: quarrelling implied an intimacy from which the fastidious shrank. Distaste for the company of her fellows, although she would not have given it as a reason since it made her seem uncaring and unaware that women and the earth (and, stretching it a bit – men) were as one, was a large part of the underlying motive for her flight to the country, and why she was now irritated by her unwonted sense of isolation. She had no desire at all to mingle with the local people. She didn't really know whether there were any.

She got to her feet, intending to announce that she

had a friend coming to stay and must busy herself with preparations, but the twins sat to her left and the large man to her right and as they made no move to let her by she sat down again, pretending that she had risen in order to shake out the folds of the tiny garment she was making. They remarked on it as it fluttered in the sunshine, showing a greater interest than you would have expected from a group of men. They were hard to understand, their accent and their form of words still strange to the outsider. When they had wrung the topic dry, using words and phrases that, in the ordinary way, Eloise would have appreciated being applied to her work, the small man spoke gravely, replacing his awesome smile with a sombre expression and saying that the time had come to be serious, to talk of Eloise, her individuality, her specialness, her destiny. She wondered if perhaps they were American, from some remote place on a plain.

Eloise was embarrassed by the attention which they pressed upon her so earnestly. They said she was wonderfully blessed to live in this hallowed place, and each waved an arm to indicate to her the specific advantages of her situation. They said many of the things that Moonbird said. And yet there was a difference. They used the same words but their meaning was hidden from her. They seemed like people trying to teach an idiot, simplifying the concepts that would always be beyond its understanding. Someone was lying to her. Moonbird or the men. They said the same things but the implications, the meaning behind their words, were unearthly distances apart. Eloise had a painful sense of the inadequacy of human language, of the depthless abysses which it strove to disguise with its meaningless precision. Even where it sought to evoke it misled, and Eloise found herself bereft even of the brief comfort of poetry. Lies. Who was lying . . .? She had a moment of clarity and then gave herself up to the meagre reassurance of confusion. She would think no more. Her mind was misted like a glass when steam rises.

'Now just glance at this,' said the small man coaxingly, opening his briefcase and flicking through leaflets. 'This page will tell you of the riches, the undreamt-of riches burgeoning unknown in your fields and hedges . . .' Eloise half listened, half dozed with the faraway look in her eyes which sometimes caused people to wonder if she was all there. She must have slept, for when she woke the garden was empty. She went into the house, her eyes clouded. Someone had left a basket of fresh herbs on the kitchen doorstep, trimmed and washed and crisp with vitality. Eloise accepted them without question. Gifts, she had always assumed, were due to her.

The cat was in the kitchen, hidden beneath the flowered skirts of the armchair. The clock had stopped, and with it, time. The watchers were back, only closer now. They were losing faith in their leading representatives.

*

'I'm home,' came the cry from the pathway. Eloise was startled. Still half asleep she looked at the clock.

'It's stopped,' she said blankly. Her routine had been spoiled, the orderly progression of events disrupted, and she felt as a card-player who had let his attention wander might feel: cheated yet uncertain as to precisely who had broken the rules. 'I must have fallen asleep,' she said, 'I just woke up.'

While Simon went to wash off the signs of toil she made a salad. She took the herbs from the basket and chopped them finely. Some she didn't recognize but they looked too inviting to reject. Once, as she crushed garlic through the press, she turned sharply to the open door with the ancient sense of being observed: her fingers tingled and, to make matters worse, the cat moaned from its hiding place. She would have called out to Simon but it seemed unwise. It is better for the hunted to keep silent: no one needs to have this explained to him. Those few remaining human instincts that are as old as man are more compelling than common sense. Eloise cracked the shell of a hard-boiled egg in her hand when, usually, she would have bashed it on the edge of the kitchen sink.

'Where's M'sieu?' asked Simon when he came downstairs, breaking the spell.

'It's under the chair,' said Eloise. 'Something spooked it,' she added, distancing herself from the taint of irrational fear. Simon bent down, lifting the frill of the loose cover to console his pet. The cat hissed at him, hurting his feelings.

'I wonder if I should get a gun,' he said, inspired by the age-old instinct to protect his nearest and dearest by force.

'I never heard of anyone shooting stoats,' said Eloise doubtfully, her own fear slowly dissipating now she had someone to talk to her in the evening hush. 'And it might be scared of buzzards.' Three of them soared daily in wide sweeps over the hill, mewing from the great height. The cat might well find this alarming; the cries of its own kind issuing from the skies above, yet knowing the air-borne creatures to be alien, not to say menacing and possibly fond of feline flesh. Human beings had long feared those others who flew without mechanical assistance. Eloise now thought that if even a kindly witch should alight on her rooftop her feelings would be mixed.

'You can't shoot buzzards,' she said. 'They're a protected species.'

'I don't care,' said Simon. In the event of a confrontation the only one he would be prepared to protect was the cat – and Eloise of course.

'Do you want me to take anything for Eloise?' asked Miriam, sunk in the embrace of her favourite white chair.

'I think she's taken everything she wants,' said Clare. The room which had been Eloise's would serve as a guest room with little rearrangement. There were none of the discarded clothes, torn posters and broken guitars which

49

characterized the rooms of most of her contemporaries.

'I was thinking more of presents,' said Miriam. 'Tights, wine, bath oil, books . . .'

'I should get some books about wildlife,' suggested Clare imaginatively. 'Flora and fauna. There's no point in buying her clothes. She doesn't wear them – not the ones I buy for her. I must have wasted about a million pounds since the time she was five.' Miriam couldn't help but sympathize. Clare's attempts to clothe her child in the acme of childish chic had been thwarted by Eloise's determination to dress as she pleased. She had worn different parts of various outfits of conflicting pattern and design in the pursuit of some image clear only to herself. Now she wore drooping, trailing, shapeless things and sometimes – Oh horror – a battered velvet hat or a long scarf knotted round her brow, gypsy fashion.

'I shall get her some little gourmet treats,' said Miriam, 'olives and bottled kumquats and violet creams from Charbonnel et Walker.' Eloise had always been reassuringly appreciative of some of the finer things in life.

'She'll like that,' said Clare, but her voice was listless and her mind elsewhere. Miriam felt that this was one of those evenings when she might as well have stayed at home with a bowl of soup. Talking to Clare when she was in this lowered mood was like playing tennis against a wall.

'You look,' she observed, 'rather as though something

had siphoned off your blood or the sawdust was running out from your seams.'

'We're getting old,' said Clare. 'We used to have fifty or sixty years ahead of us and now we haven't.' This exercise in basic mathematics coloured by pessimism irritated Miriam. As you approached forty you quite often remembered it in the night, and sometimes in the morning.

'Life is passing me by,' added Clare.

'You make it sound like a stranger,' said Miriam crossly. Clare sighed and sipped her vodka.

'Sometimes I wish I'd died,' she said. 'It would be so restful.'

'You might find it boring,' said Miriam, 'unless, possibly, you went to Hell.'

'I don't believe in Hell,' said Clare.

'Yes you do,' said Miriam. 'You believe in life after death and it follows.'

Clare in her youth, when she had been given to introspection, had been wont to explain that life was a journey to a certain destination and no matter how you travelled – first class or steerage – there was no sense in jumping ship, for if you did not sink in the disagreeably saline and shark-infested depths of the ocean, you might find yourself marooned on an arid island, or, worse, in a foreign port with dark alleyways and silent, slinking creatures and foreigners who had no intention of learning your language. Sometimes, when the gloom had sunk to inertia, Clare had said she felt all at sea and that even the prospect of eternal punishment was scarcely enough to keep her afloat.

'You're not suicidal again, are you?' asked Miriam. 'You don't have the feeling that the captain's gone home with the compass and the sextant and you might as well smother yourself in the sheets?' Clare was momentarily puzzled by this remarkable query until she realized she was being quoted: she had no recollection of using such a seafaring metaphor, but it was quite probable that she had if she'd been drunk at the time. Her father had been a ship's captain.

'I couldn't have said that,' she nevertheless protested. 'Sheets are ropes. I must've said I'd hang myself.'

'Whatever,' said Miriam. 'So long as you're not still contemplating laying violent hands on yourself.' Clare reached for the bottle.

'I said I was fed-up.' Her tone was sullen but resolute. 'I never said a word about suicide.'

'One thing leads to another,' said Miriam, 'and fed-up is nothing to be proud of.'

Clare gave voice to the hope that her friend wasn't going in for counselling among all her other good works. You never knew these days.

'Certainly not,' said Miriam, riled. 'What do you take me for?' Clare apologized.

Later that night as she lay alone in her bed she allowed herself a little desiccated crumb of comfort: she had not mentioned Claud, for whom she now had mixed feelings. Miriam had not been given the opportunity to either chastise or pity her. It was difficult to decide whether rage or regret was dominant in her emotions, and the reason was as follows.

One evening – when the day had been fine and all the restaurateurs in the city, all the café, bistro, pub owners and managers had fled on to the pavements, holding their palms upward to test for imminent rain and squinting at the heavens before bawling hoarsely at the staff to hasten out with tables, chairs, and parasols – if they had them – she had taken herself to supper. She had chosen a nearby Italian establishment with pink tablecloths and real carnations in fluted glasses, and had seated herself near the open door at a tiny table for two, electing not to sit outside because of the traffic fumes and the sweating passers-by. As she accepted the menu from an attentive waiter she glanced through the window, and who should be sitting a little way down the pavement at another tiny table for two but Claud. Here a dilemma presented itself. Should she gather up her bag, leave the restaurant and run round the block in order to approach him face to face in the most casual manner imaginable, expressing surprise to see him sitting there? No. The waiter would have found her behaviour inexplicable until he discovered her again sitting with Claud, whereupon he would cast around knowing looks and innuendo. Should she boldly summon this very waiter and instruct him to take a note to the gentleman out there in the street, at the third table down on the left? No. As she could only see the back of his head there was a remote chance that it wasn't Claud at all. Then should she rise, leaving her bag on the table, and, leaning gracefully against the doorpost, call, in a tone of amused hesitancy, 'Claud, is that really you?' No.

As she toyed with these possibilities she saw him get to his feet and, holding his unfolded pink napkin in his left hand, proffer his right to an advancing woman. Clare had sat still and not at all enjoyed her customary light repast of sole and spinach.

She had sat for some time surveying the woman as closely as she could behind a layer of glass and the faint haze of dust formed by the movement of feet and wheels, trying to persuade herself that the lady was a business associate. She did not look like a wife: wives tended to be small and plain and looked much the same. They did not present the obstacle to romance that other women did. It was a man's mistress of whom the questing female had to beware. Clare was revolted by the way the waiter fluttered around the pair, doubtless saying Italian things: he had been, in all probability, presented with a booklet of obligatory phrases at the same time as the pepper mill. Clare had chewed morosely on a bread stick until they left.

Next morning she had waited until the fairly decent hour of eleven and then telephoned Claud. He had sounded so delighted to hear her voice that it had been some minutes before she realized that he had no idea who she was. Disillusioned, she had hung up, saying there was someone ringing importunately at her doorbell. She had wept a little and been alarmed to find herself distraught at what would once have been a minor, a negligible setback. There had been times when there had seemed to be a positive surfeit of men. Now most of those who were not bound by the ties of matrimony had been once and were either hesitant to risk it again, or desperate to find anyone willing to offer comfort and companionship: these were the ones the self-respecting woman rejected, in the precarious hope of the sportsman – that the finer, elusive fish would again surface. How much longer, Clare wondered, could she afford to be selective? She had no particular wish to marry again unless a really wealthy man should offer himself, in which case it would be only prudent, but going alone to restaurants was an admission of failure. She found friendship more reliable than passion, but there was no cachet to be gained from being seen around with a female friend, especially not in a climate of consumerism, competition and market economy. It was essential to have a man in your life.

Clare thought in terms of glamour, if not romance, while conceding to the received wisdom that one's hormones were the driving force behind one's behaviour and attitude. It had not occurred to her that this conjecture, which was sometimes referred to as 'holistic', was untenable; her mind was muddled and her spirit withering and she grew increasingly sorry for herself, encouraged in this by another idea of the time – that the first purpose of womankind was to be happy. Miriam had often told her that she was unrealistic but she refused to hear. The weather had broken and the restaurateurs had bundled all the tables and chairs and the salt and pepper back indoors. Rain fell briskly on the dusty streets where they had stood, a curt reminder of the frailty and brevity of human pleasure. Clare would have been even more depressed had she thought about it, but she was asleep.

Away in the country, where the state of the weather was of greater significance, Eloise lay listening to the rain on the roof and the wind howling. It was the beginning of August, a month which, although Eloise did not know it, could be as unpleasant, in its way, as February. A month when, to the city-bred, nothing appeared to be happening except that it tended to rain and the trees grew fatter, darker and sulkier. Once, in a week's time, the quality would have been up on the moors, pursuing grouse: but the grouse had fallen victim to a form of parasite or a loss of libido and the quality, too, were much reduced in quantity.

At the moment Eloise was telling herself that the shower would be good for the garden, not realizing that the said shower might extend itself for a surprising length of time. She was thinking tenderly of all the thirsty plants, unaware that the rain would flatten the more delicate and beat the petals off the remainder. The morning would present her with a new experience. Young as she was, she did not care for new experiences:

a certain variety was welcome but anything much out of the ordinary reminded her of her relative powerlessness and gave her a sense of insecurity. Wild analysis would attribute this to the departure of her father in her formative years, but he had never spent much time with her and she had scarcely noticed when he left. Older men were irrelevant to her; creatures from another world. She got out of bed and came downstairs in the early gloom. Opening the door she stepped outside and was wrapped in mist: it felt as clinging and clammy as wet butter-muslin and made her think of death. Not that she knew a lot about death, but she did know that at some stage in the process of dissolution there would be damp cloth. Cloth was strange: man-made and steeped in ancient ritual. It was not good, this immaterial cloth that smothered and blinded her with its loveless warmth. She could dimly see the first tree in the field opposite but beyond that was nothing; all the world lost in a colourless vacuity. Eloise had never known such a thing. She went into the parlour where she kept her sewing things and held the baby dress to her face. It was dry and cool and reassuring, designed for life, not death.

'You can't go out today,' she said to Simon as he came and stood behind her. 'You wouldn't be able to see. You'd crash the van. You'd be lost.' I'd be alone, she added to herself.

'It'll go soon,' he said confidently.

'Are you sure?' asked Eloise. 'I don't want you to go

until it clears,' she said, planning a more elaborate breakfast than usual. Pancakes instead of toast.

The mist did clear, rather to Eloise's surprise: it dissipated in the valley and drifted away over the hills. Despite its evanescent form she had thought it would stay longer, might never leave. She had been subject to an illusion, mocked. Threatened? She put the possibility out of her head. At the worst the mist was only a warning, a disapproving hush and not the wild rebuke implicit in a thunderstorm. She walked round the garden, stooping occasionally to lift the broken stems, the bruised heads, thinking that Nature might be better conducted, thinking that the skies and the earth were as much in conflict as they were in accord, and it was all a bit of a mess when you *really* came to think about it. She wondered what Moonbird would have to say. Moonbird was anxious that the human race should be polite to Nature. The Native Americans (Moonbird was extraordinarily fond of the Native Americans) always apologized to trees before they cut them down, or to bears before they put an arrow through them. Eloise had asked, in a spirit of honest inquiry, whether this was for fear of reprisals and Moonbird had responded, rather coldly, that it went deeper than that. Eloise, who truly wished to understand, had not liked to probe further. It would have seemed impertinent to suggest that Nature made what an orderly mind might regard as mistakes. There was, for instance, the tree which bore gingercoloured leaves and flowers of what used to be known as corset pink. It flourished in suburban gardens in the springtime.

It was a relief to go back into the house, tidy up the kitchen and bring some order into the universe. She went round all the rooms, dusting and polishing and arranging her furniture to its best advantage. Neatness in her surroundings made her feel safe and light-hearted as nothing else did. Knowing where everything was made her happy. The dishes put away, the hearth swept, the fire laid and the mat shaken spoke of completeness and preparation for new beginnings, testament to her skill and competence; evidence that the Gates of Hell would not prevail. Hell, to Eloise, was material, physical mess. To her meticulous eye the garden, seen from her bedroom window, looked as though seven devils had passed through. There would be work for Simon when he came home. From the window of the other bedroom she looked down over the lane. There the hedgerow flowers bent low, branches lay broken in the way and sullen thistles littered seeds as though they had wearied of them. A tongue-twisting muddle of muddy puddles gleamed in the wheel ruts where the tractor had passed and there was something black and dead under the hawthorn: a crow probably. Revolting.

It was brighter and fresher when Miriam arrived the next day. Washed by the storm, the countryside had now been rinsed by a lighter rain and no longer appeared submissive, but merely obedient and a little complacent, laid out to dry.

Miriam parked her car, as she had been instructed, in the semicircular space at the bottom of the lane and walked up to the house which stood, as she had been informed, on an eminence reinforced by a stone wall. She was surprised to find that the house was made of red brick. The few others she had noted as she drove were built of grey stone, which was what you'd expect in deepest Wales. Admittedly there had been bungalows but she had disregarded them. They came in boxes and were assembled on the spot. The little red house was old and weathered, and since it stood alone did not look out of place, only different: a fairy-tale house sprung up by chance in a strange landscape. A dear little wooden gate opened on to the rising path and above it the front door stood wide open. 'Cooee,' she called, wondering briefly what others said when they arrived at an open door and were thus deprived of the opportunity to knock. Italians, Zulus, Serbs, Welshmen. What did they say? No one liked knocking on an open door. It was un-natural. Eloise came round the corner and greeted her alongside.

'I was in the garden,' she said. And she wondered, not unusually because the person who owns the door always wonders this of the expected guest, what Miriam had brought her.

'I've left everything in the car,' said Miriam, 'until I was sure I was in the right place.'

'Simon will bring it up when he comes home,' said Eloise.

'Not at all,' said Miriam, a woman of independent spirit. 'There isn't much. I'll go and get it myself.' Eloise did not offer to help but went to put the kettle on. Hostess, not host. She wondered briefly whether the word came from the same root as hostage but when Miriam came back she grew cheerful. Miriam was easy and happily full of herself, not reproachfully empty and hungry for the speech and life of others. Her square little form fitted well in the square little kitchen.

'I'll show you your room,' said Eloise, leading her up the narrow stairs. Miriam was relieved to see that there was a small but adequate bathroom and expressed herself enchanted by her bedroom, which she found charming, with never a hint of Laura Ashley or stripped pine. Dark green door, old stained floor and rose-spattered wallpaper. Willam Morris chair and small maplewood chest of drawers. Apple-leaf patterned quilt and two clean towels. She noted with approval that Eloise had stopped short of affectation and there was no carafe of water or tin of biscuits on the round bedside table. If she felt the need of sustenance in the night it was a mere hop to the kitchen.

'Well done,' she said and Eloise, gratified but truthful, said, 'I haven't changed it. Everything was here when we came. All we did was put in the bathroom and buy a fridge.'

'Didn't the last people take their things with them?' asked Miriam.

'I think they died,' said Eloise.

Such vagueness was typical of her, thought Miriam. She herself would have found it interesting to discover the history of the previous owners, their circumstances and their fate. She would have examined the deeds, gone to the records office, questioned the local people. It was sometimes said that the young should not concern themselves with the past, a view to which Miriam was strongly opposed. It gave her an image of a people going blindly forward while behind them the ground crumbled into the abyss.

Downstairs she unpacked her carrier-bag full of treats and handed them out, some to go in the cupboard, some in the obviously second-hand though functioning fridge. Savoury things and sweet things and things that shone through glass. Eloise took them as a reminder that re-wards were due to her, although she did express her thanks in the manner of a *jeune fille bien élevée*.

'I'll show you the parlour,' she said. 'We don't use it for a parlour. I keep my sewing in there.' Miriam was disconcerted by the parlour. The air hung chill and there was a faint scent of something old that had once been sweet. The furniture was uncomfortable, even to the sight. It was hard to assess in what period it had been constructed – not a time when elegance or comfort had been held in high esteem certainly. An overstuffed sofa bound in greyish cloth that might once have been blue, a square oak table with bulbous excrescences on its legs, some upright chairs and a small folding table with a brass tray on top. The fireplace was clearly unused and two unpleasant vases stood on the mantelpiece below an oak-framed looking-glass. A red and purple carpet lay on the floor and there was a pile of white linen on a puce plush armchair. On the table stood an up-to-the-minute sewing-machine looking, not arrogant in its modernity, but slightly forlorn as though at a loss as to how it had got there.

'It smells damp in here,' said Miriam involuntarily, puzzled at the contrast between the bedroom and the parlour, but feeling it would be tactless to remark on it. She could only assume that more than one person had had a hand in the furnishing of the red house and they had agreed to differ.

'I only come in to use the sewing-machine,' said Eloise, 'so it doesn't matter.' She appeared to be quite unperturbed by the room's grim charmlessness. Clare could not be blamed, thought Miriam, for whatever her shortcomings as a parent she was fussy about furniture. Eloise must have failed to pay attention while her mother, as she often did, criticized other people's deficiencies in the way of taste.

'I'm home,' came the cry from the gate. Miriam looked round.

'Does he always say that?' she asked idly.

'Well, yes, he does,' said Eloise, 'now I come to think of it.'

'Hm,' said Miriam. She had thought he might. It would be well to break him of the habit before it got ingrained. Relationships had foundered on less.

She observed Simon through the evening. He *was* a nice boy. No denying it. He was polite and thoughtful and not too domesticated. He did not thrust Eloise aside to bring the beans to the table, nor demand to know where the sauce was. He did not fall into long silences, nor hog the conversation. He had put on a clean shirt before dinner and poured out the wine with generosity and without officiousness. Definitely a nice boy. Nevertheless Miriam used the phrase reservedly: since it too often translated as *dull*. Miriam knew. Her mother had had several such young men lined up for her, which was possibly one of the reasons why she had never married.

'Your mother's well,' she stated, since Eloise had not inquired. Eloise looked mildly surprised as if at a piece of gratuitous information: it had not yet registered on her mind or emotions that there might come a time when her mother would not be well. 'The city gets her down a bit,' continued Miriam, 'but then it gets us all down in the summer.' She glanced through the window, covertly comparing what the country provided in the way of comfort with the distractions available in town. It was quiet and the air was clear, there was a lot of green about and the sheep were distantly bleating, but she could see no immediate, overriding advantage in this circumstance. Still, she'd said what the guest in the country was supposed to say and now she could forget about it. The car was there if the atmosphere grew oppressive. It was too soon to ask where the nearest town lay but she'd get round to it.

Over a bowl of gooseberry fool the directness of her nature asserted itself. 'Don't you ever get bored?'

'Oh no,' said Eloise. 'I like being by myself.' Simon considered the question.

'No,' he said at last.

'Simon's out all day,' explained Eloise. 'He goes all over the place doing all sorts of different things.' She seemed not to notice any discrepancy between her description of Simon's activities and her own admitted preference for solitude. Miriam wondered whether she was being patronizing or just ingenuous.

'Don't you ever get frightened being on your own?' she asked Eloise. 'You're very isolated.' She half regretted these words even as she spoke, but she was curious.

'There's nothing to be frightened of,' said Eloise staunchly. 'It's so far from anywhere.'

Miriam could see the sense here: there were not, after all, muggers on every street corner or stolen cars speeding round the lanes. The flaw in the maxim that there was safety in numbers had been widely recognized as people grew increasingly mistrustful of their fellows. Miriam feared that her question had been so old-fashioned as to be atavistic. She must have been thinking of ghosts and old gods, demons and things that hid in woods. It was most unlike her.

'How far is the nearest pub?' she now inquired, knowing that the pub was the centre of whatever rural community life there was left. 'Do you have friends round about?'

'Not really,' said Eloise. 'I haven't been to the pub yet.' Her voice was non-committal and Miriam wondered if she was imagining a wistful element in her remark.

'She doesn't like going out in the evening,' said Simon, 'and it's too far to walk.'

'We could go in the van in the evenings,' said Eloise, 'but Simon's always tired when he gets home.' The evidence of conflict, no matter how insignificant, inherent in their simultaneous response, gave Miriam pause for thought. She changed the subject.

'And where are the notable places of interest?' There were always local places of interest in the country. It was incumbent on the guest to express a wish to visit them and thereupon show enthusiasm ... As she brooded there was a squeal from the garden and Simon leapt from his chair to the doorway. He returned cradling the cat, whom something had upset again. It glared with rage and terror and all its claws were extended.

'Ouch,' said Simon.

'Careful,' said Miriam. Eloise went to the door and looked out.

'Something keeps teasing it,' she explained. 'Maybe a stoat.'

'Or a cat from one of the farms,' suggested Simon.

'Or a fox,' contributed Miriam.

'Or a fox,' agreed Eloise. 'Or the shepherd's dog.' They continued through the list of suspects while Simon fondled his pet, assuring it that it was safe now.

'It must be something very bold to come so close to the house,' said Miriam and Eloise shivered a little. She was thinking of the short time they had lived in the house and wondering what it was that resented their encroachment on its territory. She wrapped her dress closer round her knees and reminded herself of the words of Moonbird, who averred that a fearless, a proper woman could walk free and unharassed through the depths of the darkest forest, sail the wildest oceans secure in the knowledge of the benign concern of Mother Nature and Sister Sea.

Clare rang, when night had fallen, to learn whether Miriam had arrived safely. She sent her love to everyone.

'This jam is delicious,' said Miriam. Eloise bowed her head, more in modest appreciation of the propriety of the observation rather than the tribute itself.

'I made it,' she said. 'Would you like some toast?' Miriam had had two slices but Eloise knew that it was impolite to use the word 'more' to a guest at your table. It hinted that if the guest did not stop stuffing herself she would eat you out of house and home.

'Would you like to go out today?' asked Miriam. 'The pub for lunch?'

'Oh, I can't today,' said Eloise, determined not to

reveal herself as over-eager to escape from her fastness. 'I have to finish a nightdress and a petticoat before the end of the week and then I'll be free. You go to the pub and you can tell me what it's like.'

'Didn't Simon tell you?' asked Miriam, thinking – that's a silly question. Eloise had a way of making you ask silly questions.

'He says it's mostly full of farmers and poachers,' said Eloise. 'And the gamekeeper,' she added.

'No girls?' asked Miriam.

'He didn't say,' said Eloise. Miriam wondered if it was what would once have been called a rough pub. She doubted it. She had an impression that it was the pubs in provincial towns that were now the danger spots, full of flashing lights and the unemployed. The country pubs that she had visited were mostly run by newcomers with fancy ideas about 'cuisine'. As like as not they would hand you a plate of pâté garnished with a slice of strawberry. Even thinking about it was irritating. Miriam determined to go for a walk instead.

'Is there anywhere I shouldn't walk?' she asked. 'Anywhere forbidden to the general public?' She didn't bother to ask if the bull was quartered near since she avoided fields with cattle of any complexion, age or sex, considering it only sensible.

'I don't think so,' said Eloise, to whom the idea had never occurred. Eloise walked where she wished.

'Then I shall don stout shoes,' said Miriam, 'and head for the hills.' She had depressed herself with this inane remark and eyed Eloise resentfully, for it was her fault. She had a way of making you say stupid things as well as ask silly questions. Miriam had noticed the same tendency in some businessmen and the people you met on holiday. It meant, when you came to think about it closely, that you despised them: not deliberately, but instinctively, so that you were disinclined to offer them your true self, saving that for people of like mind and tossing those others dry crusts and cherry pips. It was not an attractive characteristic and this caused you further to dislike them. Miriam felt uncomfortable for she did not want to think of Eloise as vapid. It diminished Miriam and, by extension, Clare too. It was a great pity that Eloise's originality had been doused under the influence of Moonbird, who represented the fashion and was quite predictable with her crystals and her pyramids and her hugging of trees. She had not hesitated to point this out one evening when Eloise had brought Moonbird to Clare's flat to give her mother and her mother's closest friend the benefit of Moonbird's wisdom. It had not been a successful occasion, although Moonbird had been magnanimous and made allowances for the entrenched prejudices of the older generation. Eloise had accused her elders of ignorance and ill-mannerliness, but had sadly been already too old to smack.

'I won't be long,' Miriam announced gloomily as she went through the door. Eloise was already clearing the table wearing a concentrated expression and an air of dedication. It was extraordinarily annoying. No wonder her mother drank, thought Miriam. Eloise definitely showed signs of developing inexorably into the sort of woman who took silly things seriously. Miriam hoped she wouldn't talk too much about the planet. She found discussions about the planet futile and they usually led to Clare losing her temper.

It looked moderately pleasant from where she was standing now: green and still with biblical connotations. Being a city woman, moderately conversant with the Old Testament, Miriam thought of the countryside in terms of hills and valleys, streams and trees and flocks and herds. There they all were, open to her gaze. As she walked she became aware of the details; the uneven surface of the lane, a certain quantity of mud and the tendency of the hedgerow to fling out unexpected strands of bramble. She grew hot and took off her jacket and went on walking until the lane ended at an old gate. Sheep tracks rose up the hill in primitive terracing, while to her right and before her the hill gave way to a sudden darkened declivity, hung with trees and secretly busy with invisible, falling water. The sound slowly took precedence over the silence and then over all the other sounds, the humming of insects, the conversation of birds, the bleating of sheep.

Miriam told herself that this was peace but she found herself listening for signs of order in the rushing and heard none. If there was music here she was not attuned to it. She turned before she had intended to and walked away from that ancient, antinomian noise that took no heed of mankind.

I am clearly not a country girl, she told herself and she looked over her shoulder as though she feared pursuit. When she got to the house she was out of breath.

'I hate cows,' she said confidentially, hoping to establish some sort of rapport with Eloise, some normal level of communication. 'I could feel them watching me through the holes in the hedge.'

'They're our mothers,' said Eloise absently. She was hand sewing at the kitchen table, almost obscured by lengths of pale lawn.

'I beg your pardon,' said Miriam.

'Milk,' said Eloise. Miriam was not the woman to let an observation go unchallenged.

'What do you mean "milk"?' she demanded. Eloise thought it self-evident and looked up, faintly surprised.

'They give us milk,' she explained.

'They don't actually,' said Miriam. 'They don't *give* it to us. We take it from them.' She hoped Eloise was not now turning to Hinduism. 'They're calves' mothers,' she added explicitly. 'We're not calves.'

'No, I know,' said Eloise, seeming unconcerned by this factual statement. She bit off a length of thread and spread out the nightdress, wondering why Miriam was suddenly so cross. 'Didn't you have a nice walk?' she asked. Miriam was disarmed by her innocence and became remorseful.

'Yes I did,' she said. After all, she had not come to

71

criticize and she was instinctively aware that Eloise was, so far, glad of her presence.

'Did you see any men?' asked Eloise.

'Men,' said Miriam. 'No. Why?'

'There are four of them,' said Eloise. 'They go round the valley.'

'What for?' asked Miriam after a moment's silence.

'I don't know,' said Eloise. 'They come here sometimes.' Miriam began to think it was just as well she had arrived to make sure that Eloise was all right. She felt herself a match for any four men and wished they would appear so that she could appraise them and uncover their motives.

'What are they like?' she demanded, sitting up straight.

'Just men,' said Eloise. 'Just four men.'

'Like any others I suppose,' said Miriam, irritated.

'More or less,' said Eloise, but she wondered. They didn't seem English but nor were they Welsh. She no longer thought they might be American. They were foreign and yet, in their presence, it was she who felt out of place.

Clare woke early and went out to buy a croissant and a newspaper. By lunchtime she had grown sad and when the afternoon was well established she wept. She tried not to but there was nothing else to do and her hair was turning grey. After a while she lay on the sofa and sobbed. In the evening she thought of Italy, but then she thought of being alone abroad so she thought of Eloise and Miriam, her daughter and her friend, happily together in the country. They were breathing fresh air and eating wholesome fare and doubtlessly talking intimately and deeply about all the things that mattered. While she lay amongst the city's corruption, crying.

Eloise and Simon went to bed early, leaving Miriam to sit in the garden wondering, without too much concern, whether she had driven them away. The cat sat with her and a few moths fluttered about her head. When the telephone rang she went in and answered it. After a brief conversation she went outside again to watch the moon rise. She wondered what Eloise would say in the morning – and Simon of course.

Eloise said nothing for a while. Simon said, 'Will she be all right in that little boxroom?' Miriam nearly said that Clare could share her room but thought better of it, and Eloise said, 'Well so be it,' which Miriam considered rather dignified. 'I promised I'd meet her with the car,' she said. 'The train gets in at two.' These words brought home to them all the fact of Clare's imminent arrival.

'I'll make up the bed,' said Eloise. 'It isn't very comfortable.'

'I don't suppose she'll stay very long,' said Simon.

'I'll set off at one,' said Miriam. The day lay round them in quite a different form from what they had expected. Miriam told herself that that was life. She sat under the apple tree and read until midday. When she went into the house there was no sign of Eloise. The kitchen was immaculately tidy and clean in its threadbare fashion but Eloise was not there. Perhaps she'd gone upstairs for a nap. She hadn't appeared by the time Miriam left, but Miriam refused to worry. Nothing could have happened to her in the course of a few quiet hours and no one ran away because her mother was coming. Miriam pondered this proposition as she drove, probing it for truth.

It was hot and dry on the hillside. Eloise could hear nothing but the rustle of grass beneath her feet and she could see little because the sun shone in her eyes and the land was hazed and indeterminate. She lowered her eyes from the invisible distances and looked down and round at the wide circle in which she stood, a ring clear and well defined in the strange, drifting place where she had come without intention. She moved further over the flowered surface and in the middle of the ring she sat down and then she lay down and then she slept in the hot silence.

Miriam had to ask Clare to help put the luggage in the boot of the car. Clare was distracted and made little sense. It was now pouring with rain and the station gutters ran clear and full. Miriam had inadvertently stepped in a puddle which had soaked her foot and made her unsympathetic. Clare had not smiled in greeting and Miriam foresaw a boring drive.

'For goodness sake,' she said, 'what have you got in this case?'

'My things,' said Clare. 'I didn't know what to bring so I threw things in and came away.' She wondered briefly whether she'd remembered to lock the doors and stared piteously at Miriam through the rain running from her hair into her eyes.

'Get in the car,' said Miriam. She drove leaning slightly forward to see through the rain.

'Is it always like this?' asked Clare, rubbing at the window with a shirt cuff.

'I don't know,' said Miriam, 'I haven't been here long enough to find out. I shouldn't think so. Would you? I mean if there was somewhere where it never stopped raining I think we'd have heard. It would be a sort of record. People would write books about it and TV companies would come to do investigations. In depth.' She was too ill-tempered to point out that this was a joke and Clare was too wrapped up in her misery to notice.

'You're not being very kind,' she said, feeling a sob rising from her chest.

'I'm driving,' said Miriam. 'You can't be kind when you're driving. And it's raining. I'm seldom kind when it's raining. Nobody is.'

'You haven't even asked me what's wrong,' moaned Clare.

'I don't want to know,' said Miriam, 'not at the moment. Not while I'm driving in the rain. Unless you want to go off the road and die in a ditch.'

'I wouldn't care,' said Clare. Miriam was incensed at the selfishness of this attitude and deliberately slowed down. She had no intention of dying in her middle age just because she had such an appalling choice in friends.

'Eloise *will* be pleased to see you,' she observed grimly. Clare hiccuped. She was, for the moment, interested in the idea of dying: there was dignity in death and once you'd got it over with you were no longer in a position to make a fool of yourself. Clare was resigned to a stretch in Purgatory. Hell she still preferred not to think about. Even in Purgatory, she reasoned, she would not be lonely, for it would be full of old friends castigating themselves for not having been better conducted in their worldly term. None of them would be permitted, or desirous of, further pretence, which would make everything rather restful. Paying your debts while incurring no more would, no matter how painful, make a change from life, where it seemed that one damned thing always led to another.

Miriam, aware of the misery beside her as they splashed along in the watery gloom, although a little curious, kept the word Claud resolutely in her mouth. She didn't feel she could be bothered with Claud under the circumstances.

'Are we nearly there?' asked Clare after a lengthy silence.

'Nearly,' said Miriam. 'Do you want to play I Spy or something?' she added.

'You needn't be brutal,' said Clare, 'just because you're in a bad mood.'

Miriam drove into the bramble-hung and nettled space cut out of the field where cars were left by the few people going to the red house. 'We have to walk from here,' she said with unkind relish. The rain fell until it seemed more like a waterfall than a shower. If it went on the lane would become a river.

'In this?' exclaimed Clare on a high note of disbelief.

'You can stay here if you like,' said Miriam, 'but it isn't far.' She was no fonder than anyone else of plodding up lanes pouring muddy rivulets while the rain washed her, but it would be mildly satisfying to drag Clare in her wake.

They stumbled over the cart-tracks and slipped on the steps to the front door. Miriam pushed it open and welcomed Clare to Eloise's house.

'Where's Eloise?' demanded her mother. Miriam looked in the kitchen and the parlour and called upstairs.

'I don't know,' she said reluctantly. It was one thing to soak a tiresome parent but quite another to alarm her. 'Perhaps Simon came back and took her somewhere.'

'Was she here when you left?' inquired Clare.

'No,' admitted Miriam.

'Oh God,' said Clare.

'There's absolutely no reason to get into a state,' said Miriam. 'The rain will stop soon and then she'll be back. It was fine earlier. The weather here changes in an instant. Just remember you wouldn't be worrying if you weren't here because you'd never know she was out. She'll be back in a minute.' Clare wrung some rain from the hem of her skirt and Miriam considered lighting the fire.

'There's a Category A sex-offender loose on the borders,' declared Clare. 'It was on the news.'

'It is difficult now,' said Miriam, anxious to deflect her friend's incipient panic, 'to decide what that description denotes. It could mean merely that he opened a door for a female fellow employee or shook someone warmly by the hand.'

'No,' said Clare. 'He's a real one. He rapes people.'

'Tush,' said Miriam austerely.

Some time later (it seemed like a long time to the women who waited) Eloise came home. It was perhaps a couple of hours since Clare had arrived and she had drunk most of the vodka she had brought as a present. In consequence the worry she had sought to evade in liquor now manifested itself as temper. Eloise stood mutely before her scolding parent, turning in her fingers a strand of meadowsweet and seeming unrepentant. 'Listen to me,' insisted her mother. 'Look at you.' She was picking stalks of grass and bruised leaves of clover from her daughter's skirt, brushing at the folds in long giddy sweeps that were sometimes more like blows. Eloise reeled slightly. Miriam, thinking that, as so often, Clare's reactions were inordinate and could well become embarrassing, looked out of the window. The rain was falling as it had fallen all afternoon in its steady, inconsolable fashion. She looked back at Eloise, unflinching under her mother's fond assault. She looked at her face and thought it blind and unseemly. After a moment while the fine hairs settled on her back she took her handkerchief and wiped the girl's face. 'What are you doing?' demanded Clare of her friend, distracted from her picking and smoothing. 'What have you been eating?' she asked of her daughter. 'It looks like mushrooms,' she said and burst into tears. Perhaps, thought Miriam, perhaps she had drunk too much, was too distraught in her motherly anxiety to notice what she herself had noticed first – that Eloise, her face and her hair and her long dress, which in another place, at another time, might have appeared only ostentatious, were completely, and terrifyingly, bone dry.

'Shall I show your mother her room?' she asked. This was something she had been in no hurry for. The box-room was built out over the kitchen and could only be described as poky: it contained an iron bedstead, a bentwood chair and a chest of drawers apparently constructed from plywood. Miriam waited apprehensively for comment, but all Clare said was, 'Help,' and, 'Lucky I didn't bring much.' Miriam did not deem it worth challenging this comment. She could only suppose that her friend was still slightly anaesthetized by her afternoon drinking.

That night, while Clare ate soberingly of salted foods

79

and drank fruit juice, Miriam took an unusual quantity of wine, ate little and thought it better not to speak of water, its qualities and effects.

Simon was pleasingly patient with the two women who, it could be said, had invaded his house and his peace. Miriam knew men who would not have been so agreeable and felt warmly disposed towards him. Too well disposed to alarm him with the tremors that assailed her, her newly acquired doubts and wonderings. Nor could she speak of them to Clare, whose reactions would be exaggerated and ill-conceived. There's something funny going on, was all she allowed herself to put into so many words, and these she considered in private and not too profoundly. She had lived long enough to know the inadvisability of too much conjecture on matters for which you could find no reasonable explanation. She knew too that those who laid store by rationality (and Simon was certainly one such) would respond to her with words like 'mistake' and 'imagination', leaving unuttered the coarser terms such as 'liar' and 'mad'. It was these unspoken words which would come between companions and taint the atmosphere. You could quarrel openly with those who accused you of error or careless observation but there was little further to be said to those who thought you mendacious or unhinged. Damn it, thought Miriam. Why me, who had never the faintest interest in the occult or the untoward?

*

After a few days she had put the matter out of her mind, congratulating herself on keeping quiet and thus starving the topic of vitality.

Eloise was behaving as normally as usual, which was not, considered Miriam, as normal as her family and friends could have wished, but better than it might have been. She sometimes hummed to herself as she sewed but she always had the evening meal ready on time, vegetarian though it was and therefore demanding of more preparation than the old meat and two veg. Eloise served several vegetables and many herbs. Most days Miriam drove Clare to one or other of those places of interest scattered so liberally about the countryside: places, in the main, striving to retain their ancient character and finding to their owners' sad frustration that the only hope of doing so was by ossifying the main structure while introducing anachronisms in car-parks, toilet facilities, tea-rooms and souvenir shops. All this, of course, destroyed the point of such elderly edifices. Speaking one evening of this melancholy circumstance, Miriam used the phrase 'loss of character'. Eloise put down her spoon and said with unusual feeling that it was a wicked thing to take away a poor respectable girl's reputation on no evidence at all but . . .

'But what, dear?' inquired Miriam, after a short silence, for no one had mentioned girls, respectable or otherwise.

'What?' said Eloise, picking up her spoon and staring at her soup as though wondering how it had come there.

'You said . . .' began Miriam and then thought better of it. She found herself reluctant to pry into Eloise's mind, having had a sudden chill intimation of wilderness, of uncharted territory, drifting mists and distortions. 'I was saying,' she substituted, taking a firm grasp of the previous topic, 'that it is a waste of time to replace worn-out brick with new brick beaten up to seem old, but nor is it necessary to rip it all out and put in concrete blocks. There must be some acceptable compromise.'

'I can't see that it makes any difference,' said Clare unhelpfully. Miriam considered whether it would advance matters to develop this into an argument and decided it would not. If no one was prepared to make civilized conversation, and she was not disposed, as the only person present in full possession of her faculties, to offer a lecture, then talk must give way to silence.

'I think I shall have an early night,' she announced and went to bed. An uncertain depression kept her awake. Things unsaid and unexplained hung in the darkened room and troubled her like the suspicion of spiders. Trying to force her consciousness away from images of mist and shadow she told herself to come down to earth and then was assailed by an awareness of quicksand and precipices. As the night drew on and her uneasiness increased she realized that one cause of her disquiet was that she had spoken to no one but the inhabitants of the house since she had arrived. Even on their trips to those places of interest nobody had conversed with them. The visiting tourists were tied up in their family concerns; the immediate whereabouts of little Harry and William in this age of ubiquitous child molestation, and the pressing question of what and where to eat next. The tourists seemed all rapt in a world of which Miriam knew nothing and cared less. Nor had the owners and employees of the interesting places said anything. Miriam had ordered coffee and scones and salad rolls for herself and Clare and they had taken them away and eaten them, but she could recall no memory of chit-chat, of ordinary human intercourse.

They had been to an old mill where there were people pretending to be millers and to an old mine where there were people pretending to be miners. In the stately homes there were harassed-looking people who Miriam suspected were pretending to be the lady of the manor, although they might have been the real thing, reduced to penury and mummery, while round the lake there were people pretending to be sailors. Up in the air people flew, suspended from hang-gliders. Many were scrambling up the neighbouring mountains where some, the inexperienced or the incautious, would die in the sudden mists. Others were canoeing down rivers while yet more were pony-trekking, wearing the obligatory, unbecoming helmet. Some roamed the ruined castles, eating fish and chips and hamburgers, while, near by, their young bounced about on inflated rubber ones. Miriam was not a socialist, considering that while dictatorship meant one nasty person with power, democracy meant a lot of nasty people with power (though by no means all). Everywhere people were pretending to be people and the mountains might have been a canvas backdrop. Miriam had felt inclined to finger the grass to see if it were formed of plastic, to throw a stone at the sky to see if it bounced immediately back. The world was become a theme park and the people who thronged its artificial stage were not actors but puppets, strung along by the faceless conglomerates, the unimaginably powerful corporations that ruled the Western world. Seduced into the belief that this was the good life, the people were everywhere, imagining that they were enjoying themselves. The people believed they had taken over but it was Mammon whose interests were being so abundantly served here. The few old grand hotels had abandoned standards and equipped themselves to suit the limited and perverted expectations of hoi polloi. It was all very well, reflected Miriam, but the poetry had gone out of it. And, no, it was not well. She had no tender feelings for the upper classes, but on the whole perhaps they had done less irremediable harm than the merely wealthy. They had kept the people out of the parkland. Oh dear, said Miriam to herself, regretting the course her thoughts had taken. She wished sincerely that she could feel some warmth towards her fellow humans but she had little in common with them, and they were not, en masse, a pretty sight.

They had visited out-of-town supermarkets and spoken to no one. The checkout girl could not be engaged in conversation for she was too busy checking out and there was a queue behind prepared to erupt in rage if too long delayed before its own purchases were checked out. All human considerations were secondary to the imperative need to transfer money with all possible haste.

In only one small village had they encountered a gregarious shopkeeper of the old and vanishing kind. The shop also served as post office and off-licence and while Clare sought along the shelves for vodka, and wine labels that she recognized, the shopkeeper had engaged Miriam in conversation. 'Staying round here?' he had inquired. 'Not far,' Miriam had responded, adding and hoping that her accent was correct, 'In Ty Coch.' The shopkeeper had paused as he weighed carrots and given her an odd look. 'The Queen's house?' he had asked and had seemed about to say more when a carrot dropped from his grasp and he had stooped to retrieve it. Then Clare had asked for a box to put bottles in and he had turned to the till to make calculations. As they filled the car boot with their purchases Miriam had looked round and seen that he had followed them to the shop door and was studying them with an unfathomable expression. It had made her vaguely uneasy. She remembered that madness was infectious, like a pronounced accent, and warned herself to keep her wits about her.

In the morning she woke free from night terrors. Clear evidence, she told herself complacently, that sobriety, common sense, and an intrepid facing of one's misgivings were all that were needed to take one comfortably through life. After breakfast she went out and took up a position on the wall, determined to accost the shepherd or the gamekeeper, should they pass by, and learn something of the place and the people amongst whom she found herself. This grounding, she felt, was essential wherever you travelled on the planet, for without it you remained merely a tourist, an ignorant witness of things not understood, hampered in many cases by a superfluity of baggage that you had brought along to reinforce your sense of self in an alien environment. It was a pity, thought Miriam, that there was no one readily available to whom she could deliver this insight. They had talked about the weather over fried-egg sandwiches and honeyed toast prepared by herself. For the first time in her life Miriam felt starved of human contact and strangely homesick. Strangely because she had never been aware of having any particular feeling for what she supposed she must consider her home, a perfectly pleasant flat in St John's Wood, but not one to rouse nostalgia. Her sense of unease was slowly returning and growing stronger with the approach of noon.

There was a figure in the distance. Miriam adjusted her expression in preparation for a meeting with a fellow human, reflecting, as she waited, that the days, weeks, the passage of time had lost their customary authority; that quality of immutable measurement which dis-tinguished time in the city and here seemed not governed at all but arbitrary, even capricious. Was today, for instance, Wednesday or Thursday and did it matter? The man from the distance was now nearly level with her. He carried not a crook but a gun and so, inferred Miriam, he was the gamekeeper.

'Good morning,' she said. He stopped in the lane beneath her and looked up smiling, a smile so wide that she doubted its sincerity. 'Fine weather for the time of year,' she said idiotically. The man acknowledged this ancient gambit with tacit courtesy and made as if to move on. 'Have you the right time?' demanded Miriam hastily. As she spoke the sun emerged from behind a cloud and shone in her eyes. She blinked and shaded her face with her hand, fully expecting that when she could see again the gamekeeper would have gone on to trap predators or whatever else his purpose was on this indeterminate day.

She was surprised when she looked down to find him still there, unsmiling now, but waiting like a man under orders, for what she might demand of him. Miriam found his attitude disconcerting and half wished that Clare would appear. Clare was seldom at a loss where waiters were concerned. Waiters and watchers, thought Miriam distractedly as he gazed steadily up at her. She began to question him.

'And what did you learn?' asked Clare when Miriam described her encounter as evening fell. They were sitting in the garden close to the insect-repelling candle while Eloise was making lentil soup.

'I asked him about the history of the district,' said Miriam, sounding even in her own ears faintly self-satisfied, for it had required some effort to inaugurate a conversation with the gamekeeper. 'I asked him about the house and who used to live here and he told me all about the hills.'

'What about them?' asked Clare.

'I'll tell you if you stop interrupting,' said Miriam testily, but she hesitated. The exchange had not seemed to follow an altogether usual course, now that she looked back on it. He had not so much answered her queries as instructed her, his tone occasionally confidential but more often didactic, as though he were reciting from a manual composed unevenly of information and restrictions.

'I think he meant we must be careful,' she said at last. 'Careful where we walk,' she added inadequately.

'Insolence,' said Clare grandly. 'I bet the shooting belongs to some *nouveau riche* absentee landlord or an upstart business syndicate and they keep the wretched man to stop the public frightening the pheasants. I bet we have right of way wherever we like.' By 'public' Clare here meant herself, as her use of the first person plural partially indicated.

'I got the impression it could be dangerous,' said Miriam.

'How?' demanded Clare, her attitude growing more republican by the minute. 'How dangerous? Does he mean he'd have the cheek to shoot us or set the dogs on us or something?'

'I don't think so,' said Miriam. 'You've got him wrong. He seemed a mild sort of chap. I think he was trying to tell me the land was dangerous ... Cliffs perhaps. Or quicksands ... ' She wasn't sure whether she was referring to what the gamekeeper had said or remembering her subjective night fears. She paused again.

'You don't get quicksands up hills,' said Clare. 'If you get anything you get bogs.'

'Then bogs must've been what he meant,' said Miriam, asserting herself. 'I couldn't understand him any too well. He was funny about the house too.'

'Why?' asked Clare. 'What did he say?' She began to sound apprehensive and Miriam considered before replying.

'He seemed to think we were fortunate to be here,' she said, discarding the word 'rash' which had first occurred to her. He had worn the mildly inquisitive expression of a man who sees a stranger extracting pleasure from a situation which the observer knows holds danger.

'He probably resents us,' suggested Clare, precipitately reverting to *ancien régime*. 'Peasants are always jealous of the gentry. They think we've taken the houses from them when the fact is they wouldn't dream of living in them themselves. They like nice new bungalows with stone cladding on the outside and a utility room.' Miriam didn't bother to respond. She was thinking.

She had the impression, from what the man had said, and more from what he had not said but from something that had crept into her senses, that this had always been a house of women. Not a happy house. A house of

89

blood. The words took vivid form in her mind and she sat upright, spilling her glass into a clump of daisies.

'Careful,' said Clare, 'you frightened the cat,' and indeed the cat had climbed the apple tree and was sitting on a branch, one and a half times its usual size with its fur staring.

'Human sacrifice,' said Miriam aloud and inadvertently.

She spent the rest of the evening explaining away this unfortunate slip of the tongue as Clare pressed her for every detail of what the alarming gamekeeper had told her. She tried helplessly to explain that the discussion had been diffuse and allusive, that some other faculty than hearing or ordinary comprehension had been called into play. That the gamekeeper's words had been capable of various interpretations or of none.

'You mean you just had a *feeling*?' said Clare at last.

'That's right,' agreed her friend wearily.

'You are *hopeless*, Miriam,' said Clare.

Miriam dreamed again that night. She dreamed that the Kings were conferring together on the heights: cold Kings, incongruously dressed, wreathed in silver mist, speaking in a strange tongue. She understood not a word they said but she knew they meant no comfort to humankind. Then she dreamed that she was poaching pebbles as though they were eggs while the cat intimated contemptuously that they were unfresh. Then she stopped dreaming and slept deeply.

*

The Kings on the Hill dreamed on, but wakefully: regretting the lost days and plotting the new one.

Meanwhile the Category A sex-offender crept on his crime-strewn way across the borders.

'Simon.' Miriam peremptorily addressed her young host as he was about to leave in furtherance of his reputation as a skilled and reliable worker in wood. He had encountered a churchwarden futilely regretting the ravages that time had wrought on a rood screen and, after some assessment of his own capabilities, had judged himself the man to repair, or at least disguise, the appearance of ruin. All that remained was to convince the churchwarden and his principals that they could and must afford to employ him and he would reverse time's effects. Simon, being young and somewhat unimaginative, did not consider that time is not to be trifled with, does not rely on the present and human complicity for its existence. Time is greedy for the future, unaware that the end, like all finality, lies in its beginnings and is, in a sense, already accomplished.

'Simon,' repeated Miriam, irritated by his demeanour. Men as they leave for work have, in the eyes of women, a hint of the escapee about them. 'I want to ask you something.' Simon turned, visibly reluctant. 'I can't find us on the map.' By this she meant the precise whereabouts of the house. 'I suppose it's too small,' she continued, meaning the immediate vicinity.

'It's nameless,' said Simon carelessly, looking at his watch. 'The road's unadopted. You go by the distance from the borders.' He set off again, wondering at the incapacity of women to use the brains God gave them.

'Oh well, thanks,' said Miriam to the air, wondering what he was talking about. What, she asked herself, could be gained by considering the borders when you could not pinpoint your location? Simon, in his masculine way, was doubtless thinking of trigonometry or some such taxing discipline. Her inquiry had been purely academic, since although she had found some difficulty in travelling around the district and coming back again, she had, so far, managed it, but there was something disturbing in feeling yourself cartographically placeless. Miriam felt untypically inclined to sulk and had to make a conscious effort to compose herself. The mist had lifted from the valley and the morning was as innocent as the face of a baby. She went back into the house to the certainty of buttered toast and the whims of women.

Clare was criticizing her daughter in a peripheral and, in Miriam's estimation, a cowardly fashion. Miriam saw for the first time, quite clearly, that Clare's mode of control was not merely ineffective, but could be confidently expected to produce the polar opposite of the result it sought. She had always known and resignedly accepted that Clare went about things the wrong way, but never had she seen such obvious evidence of it. Eloise's habitual expression of obstinacy when apostrophized by her mother was now forthrightly mutinous. From the scattered remnants of the conversation, if it could be so described, Miriam gathered that Clare had been lecturing her daughter on the inadvisability of bearing a child, saying not that Eloise was yet too young, but that no woman in her right mind, if she knew what it entailed, would ever even contemplate the eventuality. From a mother to a daughter this seemed to Miriam to be lacking in diplomacy.

Fortunately Eloise was untouched by this aspect of the matter, seeing only that her mother was, as always, endeavouring to thwart her dearest wishes. Eloise was on the brink of a tantrum. Miriam, who had previous experience of these eruptions, set herself to create a diversion.

'Has anyone seen the cat?' she asked, assuming a tone and expression of nervous anxiety. 'I've been looking everywhere for the cat. What will Simon say if we've lost the cat? What shall we do?' She began to move round the kitchen, bumping into the furniture, peering under the table, dropping to her knees to look under the chair.

'For goodness sake,' said Clare crossly – too stupid, as Miriam noted, to recognize deliverance when it was offered. 'What do you care about the cat? Anyway,' she added, 'if the cat's run away it's your fault. It was you who frightened it last night. It's probably still up the apple tree.' It was purely fortuitous, thought Miriam, that Clare had survived into middle age without anyone murdering her.

'I'll go and look for it,' said Eloise swiftly, though whether from genuine concern or the decision to seize the opportunity of release, Miriam could not tell. 'Puss, puss, puss,' came the cry from the garden.

'Damn cat,' said Clare, further exasperating her friend with this unwomanly remark. Miriam began to remember what the demands of friendship normally bade her overlook, that Clare's self-centredness could become insupportable. 'What shall we do today?' asked Clare.

'You could take a walk,' suggested Miriam. 'I've noticed you putting on weight.' The unkindness of her observation was evoked by Clare's neglect of the fact that whatever she did with the day, apart from staying put, was dependent on Miriam and the use of the car.

'Oh,' cried Clare reproachfully.

'Go and look if you don't believe me,' said Miriam unmoved. It was a time when nearly every woman who breathed feared fat as she feared death and was morbidly prepared for its encroachment. 'Go and look in the mirror outside the bathroom. If you wriggle about a bit you can see most of you.' It was possible by means of tilting and adjustment to view the person in instalments, which inevitably resulted in a distorted, fragmented image, reassuring or not, according to your expectations.

'I won't,' said Clare. 'I haven't put on an ounce.'

'You're the judge,' said Miriam, shrugging her shoulders and raising her hands as though in invocation to a higher authority.

Clare, despite her native self-centredness, could not now fail to recognize that she had, in some degree, offended both her child and her friend and would necessarily be dependent for a few hours on her own resources. It seemed that a walk was inevitable even if it meant allowing the pair of them a modicum of triumph. It would be preferable to sitting alone in her room or slinking sullenly round the garden pretending not to notice their displeasure. 'I'm going for a walk,' she announced, as though an original enterprise had suddenly occurred to her.

'Be careful,' muttered Miriam, but Clare had walked out of hearing.

'Has she gone?' asked Eloise, emerging from the parlour with the cat in her arms.

'Is *that* where it was?' said Miriam, adhering to her fiction of loss.

'It was there all the time,' said Eloise. 'Has she gone?'

'Your mother is taking a walk,' enunciated Miriam. It was her role, as it had always been, to paper over the cracks in this relationship, to draw veils, make chicken soup and keep the Queen's peace. Never would she descend to an ill-natured exchange of complaints about her friend – not with anyone and least of all with her friend's daughter. Such a betrayal would cast a retrospective shadow over the past years; poison old complacencies, inflame fresh grievances and, what is more, make Miriam look a perfect fool. How could a person admit or even believe in such a waste of time and affection? How could an honest person imagine another as unworthy of her? Clare could undoubtedly be a pain in the neck, but then she always had been and Miriam had never been so immodest as to perceive her as actually inferior. Nor would she now. The person looking down on her fellows is a person out on a limb – a highly undesirable position. She bade herself forget that Clare was apt to evince this tendency.

Brooding on the nature of life and the Christian concept of the Fall of Man, Miriam washed the dishes. Advancing age brought its consolations, the sweetest being that it couldn't be too long now, but it also brought its disadvantages. Miriam found herself unwontedly clear-sighted to the failings of others and found it comfortless. It had, she mused, something to do with her inability to drink as much as she used to. That concupiscent, tolerant, vinous companionship was passing out of her grasp. She was turning, under her own eyes, into a crabby old cat. Later, powdering her nose, she was surprised to find it the nose of a still comparatively young woman.

Eloise sat under the elder tree in her preferred role of Child of Nature: she was barefoot and wore a daisy chain, already wilting, in her hair. Occasionally she sneezed and once she surreptitiously wiped her nose on the cloth she was hemming, reluctant to go to the house for a handkerchief.

The four men had come silently, without warning,

and stood around gazing at her. Eloise gazed back. Their expressions, it occurred to her, were those of professional men. Lawyers, bankers, tax inspectors, accountants, psychiatrists, all in their time had fixed her with that look: grave, expectant, waiting for her to offer an explanation or manifest a symptom. They had usually been disappointed. Eloise, who was inherently unpredictable, had learned to utilize this characteristic to advantage. By refusing to abide by or even recognize the rules laid down in these professions, she had saved herself a deal of troublesome effort and painful concentration. The mills of law, commerce, fiscal matters, usury, medicine had ground on without her assistance and had seldom proved deleterious in their effect on her circumstances. While aware that those who concerned themselves with her affairs eventually despaired of her as mentally unsound, she persisted in thinking of herself as innocent and was able, blithely, to discount their opinion. She was above all that.

Determined as she was to take life as it came and not to distract herself with tiresome detail, she did not bother to ask how it was that the men had appeared so noiselessly and, as it were, from nowhere. If she thought about it at all she assumed that they had come down from the hills, rather than up from the lane, and wasted no time in speculation. Even the fact that they cast no shadow did not, at the moment, seem worth worrying about. She waited for them to speak.

*

Miriam, who had ceased to take account of time, was still connected to the mundane by her stomach. She wanted her lunch. 'Eloise,' she said, walking round the house into the garden. 'Shall I make us an omelette?'

'What?' said Eloise.

'An omelette,' said Miriam patiently.

'All right,' said Eloise. On the grass by her foot stood a basket of mushrooms.

'Where did you get those?' asked Miriam. They were small mushrooms with long stems and pointed caps. Miriam didn't like the look of them. Eloise glanced down.

'Perhaps the men brought them,' she said. Miriam opened her mouth and closed it again. There was neither hide nor hair of a man to be discerned as far as the eye could see.

'Well, we're certainly not eating them,' she said. 'Horrible little toadstools.' They might have grown in a damp corner of Hell, she thought as she emptied the basket over the fence with a vigorous shake. 'I'd as soon fry dry rot,' she said. 'You have no idea how dangerous fungus can be.'

'Those are all right,' said Eloise. 'I've had them before.'

'In Eastern Europe,' said Miriam, 'a number of people have perished from eating the sort of fungus they'd eaten before. It had mutated, it seems, under the influence of radiation or something. It's only safe to buy them in supermarkets. Then if you die someone can sue someone.' Eloise was unmoved by this pragmatism.

'I know the safe ones,' she said, 'and the berries. All the plants.' Miriam disbelieved Eloise's statement with every fibre of her being and the full backing of her intelligence. Eloise, she thought, would be barely capable of distinguishing between a pineapple and a prune.

'What did the men want?' she asked cautiously, reluctant to encourage Eloise in either fantasy or mendacity but impelled by uncomfortable curiosity.

'I don't know,' said Eloise, looking around her. 'They left some leaflets.'

'Can I see them?' asked Miriam.

'I don't know,' said Eloise again, apparently taking the question at face value.

'I mean may I read them?' explained Miriam. Despondency was gaining on her spirits as she grew aware of the gulf between them. It would have come as no surprise to her to learn that those who committed their lives to the care of the insane were statistically more inclined to suicide than the rest of the population. 'Where are the leaflets?' Eloise passed her hand over the table where there lay nothing more than a few fallen leaves, anticipating the onset of autumn.

'There are some in the kitchen drawer,' she said, rather reluctantly, but Miriam had a way of commanding acquiescence in her wishes.

'I'll go and make that omelette,' she said resolutely. It would be a relief to beat some eggs into submission, to know that certain laws were immutable and the preparation of omelettes usually went as planned if you were willing to make allowances for occasional variations in consistency. 'Come in in five minutes or it'll go leathery.' She would use four eggs and if Clare came back she could open a tin of soup. As the butter melted in the frying pan she looked in the kitchen drawer. It contained a roll of Sellotape, a few francs, a nappy pin, an empty aspirin bottle and a layer of dry, golden leaves.

Clare had walked further than she had intended and climbed high. She stood in a glade, mossy and dappled with green-gold light. Somewhere she could hear a brook running gently without fuss or emphasis, babbling contentedly to itself. Invisible birds sang from the branches and the grass beneath her feet had a tended look, like the lawns of rich men. Clare hadn't known that nature could be so orderly. A town dweller by inclination, she had always associated the idea of nature with inconveniences such as tempests and weeds. Now she began to see why the poets had been so moved. It was really quite agreeable. She thought she might sit down and wondered idly what perversity it was that kept her from doing so. She went on standing, unaware that she was watched.

Gradually her mood changed. She had been seduced into calm by the grace of the hanging leaves, by the harebells, delicate as fragments of petrified light, the armigerous precision of the tiny, golden potentilla and the pleasingly kempt appearance of the heads of clover. Ferns, carelessly symmetrical, fringed the grass. She had felt self-sufficient and safe, content to observe without participating in, without controlling or owning the sweetness around her. Now she was assailed by discontent, for there was no one to see her pleasure, no one to whom she could reveal her appreciation and no one to buy her the source of delight. Evanescence, to a confirmed shopper like Clare, could only provoke dissatisfaction since there was nothing here to add to her collection and she must go away empty- handed. Her sense of deprivation took shape as a yearning for Claud, or if not Claud, then someone else: a prince should come walking into the glade; stately, warm and generous, and fired with love for her. Clare felt incomplete without a man. Not that she put it like that. She thought of a man, a perfect man, as a god-given right and was resentful at being cheated. It was not correct that she should be here alone and unloved in the wilderness. Her poetic sensibilities had gone into abeyance. Clare was distraught with thwarted acquisitiveness. 'I wish I was dead,' she said spitefully, to let nature know that she was not beguiled by its vacuous wiles. 'I wish I was damn well dead,' and she did sit down and she began to cry.

Among the eyes that watched her were those of the sex-offender, who had been walking all night, occasionally falling asleep under the walls and in ditches. He was tired and cross, labouring under a great sense of grievance, and he hated women. He itched to inflict some unspeakable outrage on the dreadful creature weeping in the ring and began to crawl towards her. So she wanted to be dead, did she . . .

The other watchers, who held no brief for Clare, were nonetheless unprepared to allow their authority to be usurped by a pitiful human in what was left of their domain. The Kings of the Heights dispatched him swiftly and silently and left him by the water to stare, with eyes now sightless, at the impartial sky.

They were always quick to take the opportunity of offering the unwary as sacrifice. It had grown more difficult with the advance of modernity, bureaucracy and what they loathed above all, civilization, and they were gratified at what one of their rulers, Chance, had thrown in their way. They had noticed over the course of centuries that men such as this, men who walked and lay in ditches and carried no possessions, were seldom much missed by their fellows, who did not send out parties to ravage the hidden places in search of them. They were not to know that Justice, blind but implacable, was always hell bent on discovering the whereabouts of a Category A sex-offender.

Clouds had gathered and Clare walked home under them. The watchers watched her go. They sacrificed only male flesh, and Clare in their view was past child-bearing so they had no use for her. It is interesting to reflect on what would have been Clare's reactions had she been aware of this.

It occurred to Miriam one morning that time in this place resembled the sort of book you find at the back of other people's bookshelves: long, incomprehensible and better unread. The days went by like carelessly turned pages, so that she seemed to have missed whole passages, and sometimes felt that she must have turned two pages without noticing. Life in the country when you have no occupation is often like this, but Miriam hadn't previously been aware of it and felt that something must be wrong. Eloise, for instance, was growing odder. Miriam told herself that this was not necessarily so: that Eloise might not really be changing, but that their daily proximity highlighted aspects of her behaviour which would not, in the past, have been quite so evident. But had she always spent so much time alone? Had she always had that abstracted air as though she wore invisible earphones and was listening to something inaudible to those around her? Miriam was certain that she had not habitually gone about with bits of leaf and twig adhering to her clothing, but that could just be the consequence of living close to the land and sitting on the grass and carrying in logs for the evening fire. She kept on with her sewing and cooked meals unless Miriam insisted on cooking them herself, as she did quite often because it was something to do. Clare seldom offered her services in the kitchen, maintaining that she was no good at cooking unless she had immediate access to Marks & Spencer.

They took fewer trips to places of interest, since they had been to most of them and exhausted the possibilities. Miriam could think of no historical monument that she wished to visit twice unless it had been neglected and allowed to fall into ruin. The tended ones with their brief, bright brochures carried an atmosphere reminiscent of something between school and super-market and made her feel she was being told and sold things against her will. Trivial things. History encapsu-lated, deodorized and presented on a plate – sometimes literally with painted castles and coats-of-arms. Miriam despised their unreality. There was something unreal about everything round her but in a different sense. Not the artificiality and pretence of the artefacts and souvenirs but an intangibility and something unstated. It was her urban upbringing, Miriam assured herself sensibly: a person conditioned to roads and traffic, houses and shops and crowded humanity was bound to feel alienated amidst the quiet immensity of these natural surroundings. She was only surprised that this reaction was not more generally remarked upon. People accustomed to town or country complained a little when forced to change from one to the other but seldom with fervour, never with the intensity with which Miriam felt herself burdened. It was partly the strength of the feel-ing which prevented her from making her excuses and going home. That would be irrational and therefore neurotic, and Miriam scorned neurosis.

Clare, insulated by her private grief and resentment, was untroubled by these external matters. Alone on a desert island or crammed into a shopping mall she would have been conscious merely of her own condition. Miriam wasn't sure whether this were enviable or not.

Perhaps not, judging by her demeanour. Clare did not look well. When she spoke it was apparent that she was expending upon herself a quantity of compassion that would not have come amiss were it directed to a whole community of lepers. Discussing her afflictions, which now included a summer cold, her voice took on a low, serious timbre, and her face an expression of earnest perplexity. No government minister addressing the plight of homeless children could have evinced a deeper concern. This drove Miriam to adopt a show of unnatural cheerfulness which was tiring to sustain.

It was almost a relief when the policemen called. They were looking for the sex-offender, whose trail of rapine and pillage had stopped abruptly at the border and of whom there had been no further trace. They were circumspect and strove not to alarm the ladies unduly, but it was obvious that they suspected him of having gone to ground somewhere in the hills and woods of the district. Miriam gathered that the inhabitants of this remote homestead should be vigilant, report any sightings of a stranger, while under no circumstances confronting him, and should lock the doors and windows at night.

The watchers turned their cold gaze from the activity of the uniformed interlopers and regarded their Kings. There was an early frost that night in the valley.

For a while a police helicopter disrupted the ordinary routine of the raven and the buzzard. Had they been left to pursue their accustomed ways a keen observer might have learned from them where the carrion lay concealed, subject now only to the ministrations of the earthbound attendants of the dead. The maggot and the ant did as nature bade them, untroubled by competition from the air, and there was no human eye to see.

Clare was momentarily diverted by the presence of the police, which gave her a sense of security. It was only when they left that she fully realized the reason for their presence and gave herself up to unease.

'Do you think we should go back to town now?' she asked.

'And leave Eloise on her own all day?' inquired Miriam.

'No, of course not,' said Clare. 'I meant we should take her with us.'

'I doubt if she'd come,' said Miriam. 'Besides,' she added, speaking of the sex-offender, 'he's probably there himself by now. Criminals prefer the town to the country.' Clare was silent for a moment.

'Why?' she asked.

'Why what?' said Miriam who had spoken without thinking. Their roles were briefly reversed.

'Why do criminals prefer town to country?'

'They like the company,' said Miriam shortly, her mind still not on the subject. Clare thought again, frowning and circling her finger in a drop of red wine which had fallen on the table.

'Some of them might,' she said seriously, 'the ones

who go round in gangs and have wives and mothers, but I shouldn't think rapists do. They must like a bit of privacy.' Miriam called her mind to order. It had been wandering again in unaccustomed places, misty and nightmarish. 'I don't like the thought of him,' concluded Clare. It was unfashionable to confess to fear unless you were being threatened by a man you knew personally. Women were expected to be sensible about social concerns and to take into account a misfit's background. Atavistic terror of the unknown was not considered a proper response. Not that Clare had thought it out but she was not immune to the climate of opinion.

'All rapists have mothers,' said Miriam, 'and some of them have wives.'

'You know what I mean,' said Clare, assuming, as most people do, that failure to agree with her was indicative of deliberate perversity rather than the result of a different process of thought.

'I wasn't listening,' said Miriam. 'What were you saying?' but Clare had thought of something else.

'You know the day I got here,' she began, and paused.

'Yes?' said Miriam.

'You know how – odd – Eloise was?'

'Yes,' said Miriam.

'Well, do you think something might have happened to her?'

'No,' said Miriam, suddenly seeing where this was leading. Clare's fondness for drama was always exacerbated by boredom and she had undeniably been suffering from the uneventful nature of country life. It was not enough for her to know that there was a rapist at large in the vicinity. She was intent on bringing him closer, on acquiring some personal interest, if only by means of speculation. Miriam found this unhealthy but she waited for Clare to incriminate herself before giving her opinion. If she spoke prematurely Clare would deny any such intention. She gazed at the fireplace.

'Are you sure?' asked Clare rashly.

'Sure of what?' demanded Miriam in a deceptively gentle tone.

'Quite sure that . . .' began Clare, and Miriam could restrain herself no longer.

'If you're suggesting that your daughter was attacked by a mad rapist and neglected to mention it,' said Miriam, 'then I believe you are doing her an injustice.'

'I wish you wouldn't talk like that,' said Clare. 'You sound as though you'd been reading something.' Miriam's superiority of intellect had always been a slight source of grievance except when it came in useful. 'I wasn't going to suggest that. I was just wondering if she'd seen him . . .'

'That would hardly have upset her,' said Miriam. 'Just seeing someone.'

'But you admit she was upset,' said Clare. 'You just said so.'

'*You* were upset,' said Miriam. 'She was . . .' and here Miriam paused, for she had been going to say 'bone dry' and she had determined never to mention it.

'I was only upset because she was upset,' claimed Clare, and since the conversation promised to go round in circles Miriam put a stop to it.

'We're going to drive down to the pub,' she announced, 'and have a change of scenery.'

'We can't leave Eloise,' protested her mother.

'We're not going to,' said Miriam. 'We're taking her with us.'

'Oh,' said Clare. Fond as she was of her child, she found her a no more convivial drinking companion at eighteen than she had been at eight. She and her daughter were different sorts of people.

'Eloise,' called Miriam. 'Where are you?'

'She was in the garden earlier,' said Clare.

'Then she's probably still there,' said Miriam, and she went out to look for her.

The pub, flat-faced and unremarkable to the passer-by had, inside, the shadowy coolness found only in country dwellings and places of refreshment; it seemed larger than was likely from its outward appearance. Numerous small rooms led into others, descending by several flights of steps to a back door which opened on to a river bank, where the landlord kept crates and boxes and various objects the utility of which would not be obvious to the casual observer.

'Where shall we sit?' asked Miriam, leading the way to a table and benches in a lower room lit by a dim window high in the wall.

'Why don't we sit here?' said Clare as she followed. Her spirits had risen a little at the ambience of wood and tobacco smoke which stained the walls and beams and, it seemed, the air. 'I love the smell of stale beer,' she said.

'You hate the smell of stale beer,' said Miriam.

'Not today I don't,' said Clare. 'I'm sick of the smell of fresh air.' But already melancholy was creeping over her again.

'I'm hungry,' said Eloise. These were the first words she had spoken since Miriam had found her outside the garden, staring up at the wooded hill, and had led her to the car.

'I'll get a menu,' said Miriam, turning back up the steps.

'I want a steak,' said Eloise.

'You're a vegetarian,' said her mother. Miriam left them to it and went to the bar. They were the only customers in the pub and it seemed at first that the place was also empty of staff.

'Is there anybody there?' she demanded loudly, rapping on the bar counter.

'He'll be up in a minute,' said a voice. Miriam jumped. The man must have come in silently and taken up his place in the far corner. He hadn't been there when they came in.

'Where is everyone?' she asked.

'Down below,' said the man. Miriam regarded him more closely, peering through the dimness.

'You're the gamekeeper,' she said, pleased to be able to

recognize him out of context. 'We were talking the other day.' As she spoke she remembered the somewhat unusual tone of the conversation and reprimanded herself for what she now considered to have been a lack of attention. She had, Miriam told herself, heard the kind of thing she had half expected to hear. She had not listened closely but had let her imagination run away with her. She had not been fair. 'So how are you?' she asked, resolutely set on listening to what he might say, determined that his accent should not affect her concentration. She would listen to the words and not the inflexion.

Then the landlord appeared, rearing up behind the bar. Miriam jumped again. 'May we see the menu?' she asked nicely, and heard herself adding, 'I'll just ask the girls what they want to drink.' There was something repellent in his demeanour. 'Vodka, Clare?' she called. 'Lemonade, Eloise?' There was no response. She went to the top of the steps and asked again. The two of them were sitting quite still, unspeaking. 'What do you want?' she called, too loudly. It seemed, when they finally answered, thought Miriam, as though they were coming out of a trance.

'There isn't a menu,' she said, 'because I gather there's nothing to put on it.' She sat down and took a mouthful of vodka. At the prompting of the gamekeeper the landlord had grudgingly offered to compose a plate of ham sandwiches. Miriam had explained, smiling, that one of her party was vegetarian, one Jewish and one slimming, and had bought a packet of crisps. They were stale.

'What a rotten pub,' said Clare. She swallowed her vodka and Miriam went once more to the bar, preferring to play Hebe rather than sit wondering whether Clare was insulting the innkeeper. Being rude in the country was worse than being rude in town where bad manners went largely unnoticed. Here, she knew, an offensive remark could have long-lasting consequences. She could think of no bucolic phrase to initiate a conversation and asked the gamekeeper, outright, who used to live in the house which Eloise and Simon considered their own.

'The Queens,' he said, and then amended this to 'The ladies.'

'What ladies?' asked Miriam, unwilling to pursue the mysterious royal connection. The gamekeeper looked weary and Miriam wondered uneasily if he had told her already, on the occasion when she had neglected to concentrate. 'I'm getting *so* absent-minded,' she confided untruthfully. Yet already she felt her attention wandering, the darkness of the pub seeping into her eyes, into her mind; his voice far, his words distinct but meaningless . . .

The Kings' women had been lost, taken, long ago before time or words could tell, before the forests fell or the mists lifted.

'Goodness,' said Miriam with an effort. He spoke softly and she could not decide whether it was mesmerism or manners which kept her leaning against the bar, listening.

Driving back to the house she hummed under her

breath. Since Clare didn't tell her to stop it, she ceased of her own accord and spoke to break the silence. 'We'd better have something to eat,' she said, 'when we get back.'

'I want a steak,' said Eloise again from the back seat. Her mother said nothing, so Miriam said that if that was what she wanted, it was probably her body telling her she needed the elements that red meat would provide. It was not the sort of thing she would have chosen to say, but with the present dearth of intelligent conversation it was all she could think of. She scowled.

'You know there isn't any steak,' said Clare. 'There's only some tinned ham in the back of the cupboard.'

'Then I'll have that,' said Eloise composedly.

'If you wanted ham,' said Miriam, 'you could have had sandwiches in the pub. Why didn't you say?' Eloise considered for a while.

'I thought the landlord's hands were probably dirty,' she explained.

'You didn't even see the landlord,' said Miriam.

'Men's hands are usually dirty,' said Eloise.

'That's a very sweeping statement,' said Clare, who was reviving now that she was out of the atmosphere of the pub. 'I have known men with very clean hands and neat cuticles.'

'Hairdressers,' said Miriam. 'Surgeons . . .'

Clare agreed. 'Men who spend their working lives up to the elbows in people's insides have to wash their hands to get the blood off. It dries under your fingernails if you're not careful.'

'Chefs,' suggested Miriam.

'Chefs are filthy,' said Clare.

'Who told you that?' asked Miriam.

'I can't remember,' said Clare. 'Somebody. They have bits of potato peel and prawn shells stuck in their pockets and their aprons are stiff with blood and sweat and tears – and dripping,' she added.

'We mustn't seethe the kid in the milk of its mother,' said Eloise, startling her elders.

'We weren't proposing to,' said Miriam, 'so I wouldn't worry about it.'

'Cruel,' said Eloise, 'to boil a little baby in its mother's milk.'

'Do shut up, darling,' said her mother. 'You're depressing us.'

'You always refuse to face facts,' said Eloise. Neither Miriam nor Clare could think of a response to this: as far as they were aware no relevant facts had been under discussion.

That had been, thought Miriam, one of their sillier conversations. She and Clare occasionally had really silly conversations, but usually when they had stayed up late and drunk rather too much. And why, she asked herself, was Eloise's mind running on the dietary restrictions of Deuteronomy. It must be that she harboured some feelings of guilt about her lapse from vegetarianism: being Eloise she would not express these feelings in the ordinary way but would direct them into arcane channels where it was difficult to follow. Miriam tried to remember whether she had ever tried to instruct Eloise in the requirements of the kosher kitchen. She supposed she must have done.

'Eloise,' said her mother, 'you're away with the fairies.'

'They call them the Tylwyth Teg round here,' said Miriam off-handedly.

'I'm home,' called Simon. The women sighed. Clare loudly, Miriam imperceptibly and Eloise regretfully. She was in the garden in the quiet of the evening and she did not feel lonely. It had seemed right that there were women in the house while she was alone by the woods. She sat still.

'What's that bruise on your head?' asked Miriam suddenly. There was a nasty contusion on Simon's left temple.

'It's nothing,' said Simon. 'I was mending a gate and a tree fell on me.'

'I don't call that nothing,' said Miriam.

'I was only caught by a branch,' said Simon. 'I'd just stood up and I was moving away when it came down. It was a rotten old tree,' he explained.

'Where's M'sieu?' he asked, taking off his boots seemingly unconcerned by his accident.

'Eloise is in the garden,' said Clare, considering that

his first query should have concerned the whereabouts of her daughter.

'Is he with her?' asked Simon, and he called, 'M'sieu, M'sieu.'

'It's under the chair,' said Clare irritably. 'Probably sleeping off the birds it's been eating.'

'He doesn't eat birds,' said Simon fondly, bending down to see his cat.

'Then I wonder who left the pile of feathers in my room,' said Clare. 'I just went up and they're all over the floor.'

'But I closed all the doors before we went out,' said Miriam, 'so he couldn't sleep on the beds.'

'A bird must have come in through the window,' said Simon.

'And plucked itself?' suggested Clare. Simon got to his feet.

'I'll go and pick it up,' he said.

'What a good boy,' said Miriam, 'he doesn't make a fuss,' and she wondered when she had last heard the phrase 'a wonderful man'. It was never used now. Women were often described as wonderful, usually for somewhat insufficient reasons, but men were not, even when they behaved well.

'What are you dreaming about?' asked Clare: she was hoping Miriam would think of something nice to make for supper.

'I was thinking about men,' said Miriam.

'I thought it was me who did that,' said Clare, an

image of Claud forming in her mind. She was no longer troubled by the urge to discover his house and sit on his doorstep, but she was still regretful that nothing had come of their meeting. He had seemed so suitable.

'I was addressing myself to some of the more profound, underlying aspects of the relationship between the sexes,' explained Miriam.

'You must tell me all about it,' said Clare. 'What shall we have for supper?'

'You never used to talk about food all the time,' said Miriam. A reply could only have been undignified. Clare reached for the vodka.

'Yet they still have power,' brooded Miriam. 'Not just the obvious sort which could be denied them – politics and business and law – but the power that women allow them.'

'You mean they can make the first move,' said Clare, thinking that if she had pounced on Claud during the dinner party he would, in all probability, have fallen back, aghast. Men did not like to see their predatory instincts reflected in women. It gave them a fright and they did not find it complimentary – only unnatural. It wasn't fair.

'There is that,' agreed Miriam. 'One of the greatest differences between the sexes is that women are sometimes moved to love by a show of desire, even from a man who is not, on the face of it, highly desirable in himself. Whereas a man may be flattered by a floozie flinging herself at his head, he takes it simply as an acknowledgement of his virility and charm and his emotions are not stirred. Now a woman may fall in love with a man merely because he lusts after her. She, poor thing, thinks that he loves her.'

'I can follow that,' said Clare moodily. 'What I can't understand is the people people marry.' Miriam was aware that in her role of sensible person she was expected to chide Clare for exhibiting prejudice but she declined to do so.

'I quite agree,' she said. 'It makes me think I don't understand human nature at all.' Clare was gratified if mildly surprised.

'I thought you'd say they saw the beauty of each other's character,' she ventured.

'Why would I say that?' said Miriam. 'It can only be that people vary in their tastes. Maybe to some, fat ankles or cross-eyes are exquisite. Who knows?'

'Film stars don't look like that,' objected Clare, 'or models, or the people rich people marry.'

'Maybe,' said Miriam. 'Who cares?'

'Market forces,' said Clare vaguely. 'It must be all down to supply and demand or something.'

'Anyway,' said Miriam, 'I wasn't thinking about that aspect. I was thinking that, with a couple, the woman sinks – or rises, of course, should she be so lucky – to the level of the man's social expectations.' She was remembering a day some years before: a time when Clare had conceived a passion for a minor politician. He had invited them both to accompany him to lunch at the house of one of his friends. There had been many people present and Miriam, who sprang from intellectual stock, had never previously endured such an experience. The principal characteristic of the occasion had been sexual innuendo combined with a strong strand of competitiveness. She had met, as far as she could gather, businessmen, and women, a few social workers, a doctor or two and some other minor politicians. Seldom had she felt so out of place. Few of them had read a book, unless they had acquired one from an airport bookstall on their way to some destination where they would encounter others like themselves, and they spoke exclusively in the current clichés. Their host and hostess had subscribed to that school of thought which holds that if you order things in the home much as they are ordered in the hotel, then you can't go far wrong, and, in their bathrooms, the end of the lavatory paper which presented itself for use was folded into an arrow head. Miriam had sidled away before lunch, leaving Clare talking to a high-heeled blonde who was clearly asking herself who Clare thought Clare was.

The following day Miriam had explained that she had left early, not because she had had a headache or felt faint, but because the choice and quality of the reproductions which had hung on the walls of the house of the politician's friend had wounded her aesthetic sense. 'Do you remember that politician?' she asked.

Clare did not trouble to dissemble. 'Enough,' she said.

'You thought he was wonderful at one point,' Miriam reminded her.

'Not wonderful, no,' said Clare. 'He had a nice car and I thought he was rich enough to match but he wasn't.'

'You're not fair to yourself,' said Miriam. 'That is, if mercenary motives are as reprehensible as we are told. It is never merely their money that attracts you. It is something else, only I can never tell quite what.'

'You don't have the eye,' explained Clare, 'but you were right in this case. He wasn't . . .'

'He was a nightmare,' said Miriam.

'I was going to say he wasn't quite a gentleman,' said Clare. 'I did realize in time. Anyway, why were you thinking about such a boring thing?'

'I was thinking,' said Miriam frankly, 'that Eloise could have done much worse than take up with Simon. He's not rich but neither is he vulgar.'

'That's probably why,' said Clare. 'He's not vulgar because he's not rich and he's not rich because he's not vulgar.'

It had grown dark. Darker than dusk. Simon had come downstairs with a dustpan full of feathers. He had heard the conclusion of their conversation and looked grave as he went, without speaking, into the garden.

'We've shocked him,' said Clare. 'He thinks people don't talk like that any more.'

'He's led a sheltered life,' said Miriam. 'The young tend to mistake vulgarity for innocence.' Simon would not have judged the politician's friend if he'd caught him eating peas with his knife – he'd just think he was unaffected and unspoiled. 'Good manners are regarded as elitist,' she concluded.

'So if he thinks we've been rude he ought to be pleased with us,' said Clare.

'It doesn't work like that,' said Miriam. 'The mob can be rude to us but we can't be rude to them. That's tumbrel talk.'

'What are you doing?' asked Eloise, walking on silent feet through the gloaming. Simon started and dropped the trowel. 'I'm burying this bird,' he said.

'Oh, the poor thing,' mourned Eloise, kneeling down to stroke it. 'But there isn't a bird in there,' she said, 'only feathers.' Simon said nothing. He had been wondering where the body of the bird had gone and could only suppose that M'sieu had indeed eaten it. Miriam must have left the door ajar.

'Go inside, Eloise,' he said. 'It's cold and it's going to rain.' Eloise raised her head and looked around. She was sniffing the air.

'No it's not,' she said. Simon drew back. There was something inhuman in her attitude, her head inclined towards the evening breeze.

'Eloise,' he said. She relaxed slowly and brushed her black hair away from her face, flower pale in the dusk, now no more fleshly than the blossoms of convolvulus hanging in the sudden stillness. 'I wish . . .' he said.

'I wish,' said Eloise, 'I wish, I wish . . .' But Simon did not want to know what his love wished. He refused to know. He shut his ears and turned to the house.

'What's the rush?' asked Clare as he almost stumbled in. She looked at his face. 'What's the matter?' she said. 'What's out there?' But only Eloise followed him through the door. Nothing else. All the same, Clare closed and locked it.

'No sense in taking chances,' she observed.

They had nearly finished supper when the knock came. Eloise was eating up the tinned ham.

'Don't gobble . . .' her mother had begun, wondering distractedly what had become of the refined little girl and the vegetarian teenager. Simon, as startled as anyone, banged his hip against the table as he went to answer the knock.

'It's the police again,' he said. 'Different ones.' There were, as is often the case, a big one and a smaller one who smiled; and in the lane, barely visible as night drew on, were two more with an impassive expression who appeared indistinguishable, one from the other. Clare and Miriam went out to discuss the situation with the arm of the Law, but Eloise sat at the table, slowly chewing.

'I thought he'd passed on,' she heard her mother saying shrilly. 'I thought you'd chased him back over the border.' The response was inaudible and Eloise ate another bit of ham: she was only eating what would have been Miriam's share. Then she heard the door close and the others came back into the kitchen, Clare complaining about the misuse of her taxes and the incompetence of our much-vaunted police force. Miriam sat down again.

'How many policemen does it take to make a single inquiry?' she asked without expecting an answer.

'They always go round in twos,' said Clare.

'There were four of them,' said Simon, and then was assailed by an uneasy sense of *déjà vu*.

'He must be very dangerous,' said Clare, 'the rapist.'

'Moonbird says all men are rapists,' contributed Eloise in a conversational tone. Her chin was greasy. Clare shrieked, frightening, among others, M'sieu. Miriam dropped a spoonful of lightly boiled egg and Simon knocked over the stool.

'Don't do that, Clare,' said Miriam. 'You almost gave me heart failure.'

'Eloise,' said her mother, 'if you mention that mad woman's name I shall . . .'

'Go home?' suggested Eloise indifferently.

'There's no need to be offensive,' said Clare, regaining control of herself. 'Nothing would persuade me to leave you while there's a rapist prowling round.' She hadn't said that for effect, noted Miriam approvingly. She meant it.

'He isn't here any more,' said Eloise. 'They . . .' She was silent.

'Who?' said Miriam and Clare simultaneously said, 'What?'

'Who do you mean by "they"?' asked Simon gently.

'Oh, I don't know,' said Eloise, yawning. 'I forget.'

'For God's sake go to bed,' said her mother, exasperation mounting again. 'I don't think I can stand much more.' Miriam sighed regretfully. Her friend's undoubtedly genuine concern for those she held dear was always eventually superseded by care for herself.

'Come, my chickens,' said Eloise, 'up the wooden hill to Bedfordshire.' Simon followed her but Miriam had a distinct impression that it was not he whom Eloise had addressed. She stared after them. Clare was staring too.

'Where the devil did she get that from?' she said. 'I never taught her that. Did you?'

'Certainly not,' said Miriam. 'It must've been you.'

'Well it wasn't,' said Clare. 'If I hadn't been there at the time I'd doubt whether it was me who gave birth to that girl.'

'It was you,' said Miriam. 'Believe me. I was there too.' She looked as though she might be about to say more.

'All right,' said Clare. 'You don't have to remind me.'

During the next few days Miriam lay in wait for the gamekeeper.

'Why are you sitting there?' asked Clare one morning, finding her friend seated uncomfortably on the wall overlooking the lane, her legs dangling.

'I'm admiring the view,' claimed Miriam. 'From this angle it has a particularly Welsh feeling.' For a moment Clare stood beside her, studying the aspect.

'How do you make that out?' she asked eventually, loth to admit that to her the fields looked like any others in the northern hemisphere, innocent of national stamp or characteristic.

'It's a very ancient landscape,' explained Miriam. 'That outcrop of rock down there is far older than any to be found over the border, and that long narrow stretch where the grass is greener is where they dragged a dragon from the mountain top, where the Kings had killed him, to the lake at the bottom of the valley.'

'There isn't a lake,' objected Clare.

'They drained it,' said Miriam. 'The dragon transmuted into a *ceffyl dŵr.*'

'A what?' said Clare.

'A water horse,' continued Miriam, 'and it terrorized the local inhabitants, rearing up and shattering the doors of their houses with its scarlet hooves, so they emptied the lake and he sank into the mud. That darker bit down there where the reeds grow, that's where he lies.'

'You made that up,' accused Clare.

'Would I waste my time making something up?' demanded Miriam. Clare bent to stare into her face.

'You're not going to tell me it's true?' she inquired.

'I didn't say that,' said Miriam. 'I said I didn't make it up and somebody . . .'

'Told you,' said Clare.

'. . . told me,' concluded Miriam.

'Who?' asked Clare. Miriam hesitated.

'Someone I was talking to in the pub,' she said at last, for she was not really sure where she had heard this improbable tale nor why she knew it so well.

'The only one I've seen you talking to is that game-keeper and I can't understand a word he says,' protested Clare.

'It is difficult,' admitted Miriam. Since he spoke Welsh part of the time it was necessary to cling to the context in order to keep up and be able to nod sagely when the gist became apparent. She thought he must be a rarely skilled story-teller, for some of the images he had evoked were startlingly clear in her mind despite the difficulties in communication. She wondered again whose game it was that he kept and where he walked before he came down the furrowed lane and where he went afterwards.

'I'm going for a rest,' said Clare. 'I feel terrible.'

Miriam made no answer but continued to wait.

Then he came as she had known he would. He stopped and looked up at her and she leaned down.

'Tell me again,' she said, 'about the women who have lived in this little red house.'

Miriam opened the door to the parlour. A newly made nightdress lay negligently over a chair. It looked, she thought, as though it might get up and walk if she startled it. She picked it up and threw it down untidily so that it seemed only like a crumpled piece of cloth. She had heard the sewing-machine whirring in the night and concluded that Eloise had been unable to sleep. No wonder she looked tired. The room smelled faintly of that old scent; a scent that, once familiar, might remind a child all through life of its mother's touch. Might frighten it into fits, she thought. She went to open the window but it was warped and immovable. Perhaps in most houses, thought Miriam, there were rooms that were better left unused. It was cold in there. She went back to the kitchen closing the parlour door firmly behind her.

'Do we believe in ghosts?' she asked.

'No,' said Clare.

'We don't believe that people can leave impressions of themselves in the walls, in the air that they used to breathe? Influences in the very atmosphere?'

'No, of course not,' said Clare. 'Don't be silly.'

'Dim shapes in doorways, words echoing down the stairway?'

'No,' said Clare.

'I am not as certain as I used to be,' said Miriam.

'You're being very annoying,' said Clare. 'If I'd said I believe in ghosts you'd've laughed at me.'

'You're more gullible than me,' said Miriam. 'I'm suspicious of your enthusiasms. This is different.'

'What's different?' asked Clare. 'You're not telling me you've seen something?'

'I've heard something,' said Miriam. Clare looked at her nervously.

'Heard what?' she demanded, apparently prepared to

be persuaded of the existence of ghosts if Miriam should insist on it. Miriam wished that her friend could be relied on to take an independent view and that they could discuss the matter without it leading to hysteria.

'I've heard a story,' she explained, 'nothing more.'

'You've been listening to that man again,' said Clare, enlightened. 'I thought you were more sensible.' Miriam was reassured by this down-to-earth observation and thought that perhaps she had underestimated her friend. There was an aspect of human relationships too infrequently taken into consideration, whereby the weak faced by doubt in the strong momentarily assumed the dominant role. It could work for good as well as ill.

'This has always been a woman's house,' she said. 'Men never thrive here. That's why no one lived here for all those years. The men always died or something.'

'Simon looks all right,' said Clare robustly, but she added, 'What something?'

'The cat doesn't like it here,' said Miriam.

'Damn the cat,' said Clare. '*What* something?'

'They went mad, or committed suicide or disappeared in the hills – all sorts of things,' said Miriam. 'Ty Coch stands on an old sacrificial site and the locals won't live in it. It's always gone to strangers in living memory and before that and as long as they're only women . . .'

'What?' asked Clare.

'They're more or less all right,' concluded Miriam lamely. 'Three women lived here until the last one died.'

'When?' asked Clare in her new incisive tone.

'Oh, years and years ago,' said Miriam.

'And what happened to them?' inquired Clare.

'They died,' said Miriam. 'I just said so.'

'I mean when they were alive,' said Clare.

'I don't know,' said Miriam.

'Well, that's some story,' said Clare contemptuously. 'I could tell a better one myself. Didn't you ask him what happened?' Miriam hesitated. She had found she had no wish to know what happened. Like someone who is approached by a messenger wearing the expression common to all bearers of ill-tidings, she had endeavoured to change the subject before it arose. Even as he spoke – of scandal and illegitimacy and infanticide – she had tried to think of other things, for behind his commonplace, if regrettable, account there lay a hint of something stranger and darker, something that no mortal should be asked to comprehend. There were unsuspected depths here, layers of dreadful mystery that should remain hidden from human awareness; and from some forgotten time there drifted into her consciousness vague memories of tales of a world of chaos, of the demiurge and invincible evil.

'There are worse things than ghosts,' she said. Ghosts suddenly seemed much closer to everyday reality and hardly to be wondered at. One step as they were from mortality, they seemed, by comparison with the unknown, almost cosy. 'The house is haunted,' she went on more confidently, 'but it doesn't matter.'

'*I* have seen nothing,' said Clare, implying, rather obviously, that if a person of her sensitivity and delicacy of constitution had not been compelled to endure a sighting, then there was nothing to be seen.

'You haven't been looking,' said Miriam, declining to comply with her friend's assessment of her own psychic capabilities. Clare was affronted but, as so often in their relationship, powerless to respond satisfactorily.

'You've been seeing things,' she said crossly. 'You were probably drunk.' Miriam, ashamed of her easy assumption that Clare would respond to talk of phantoms with a fit of the vapours, did not argue but resolved to shake herself free of a little intellectual superiority.

'So what do you think?' she asked humbly.

'About what?' responded Clare, still cross. 'If you mean do I think Eloise is possessed by the spirit of some old Victorian female, the answer is no.' She cast Miriam a challenging glare but Miriam was too surprised to say anything for a moment. She could hardly have been more disconcerted if M'sieu had suddenly uttered an opinion on the origin of species. In all the years they had been friends, she had never imagined that there were abstruse matters about which she and Clare might have identical thoughts. She felt as though she had pulled a cracker and found not a joke inside, but one of her own more profound insights. How very salutary, she thought as she strove to adjust to this new perception.

Clare was regretting her words. She had travelled lazily through life by often responding with a show of incomprehension to questions which might threaten her comfort by demanding a resolution. Other people, thereby, had been constrained to look after her. If she were now convicted of greater intelligence than she had admitted to, then much support would be withdrawn. Besides, she had long been accustomed to deny reality by refusing to consider it. It seemed easier. If people believed you incapable of turning a key then they did it for you. Now she felt strange. She had voiced a fear which should have been left unuttered.

'I can always tell what you're thinking,' she claimed, retreating uneasily from her unwary step into exposure. Miriam caught her back.

'Then what about those things she says?' she demanded. 'Those phrases she uses. Where does she get them from?'

'Oh, Moonbird probably,' said Clare.

'I doubt if Moonbird uses that type of anachronism,' said Miriam. 'Moonbird talks New Age.'

'She's probably rocked her brain loose, dancing in all those circles,' said Clare, brightening at this shift in the topic of conversation.

'Stick to the point,' said Miriam remorselessly.

'If you must know,' said Clare, capitulating, 'it did cross my mind that we should consult an exorcist, only it seems so extreme.'

'Not an analyst?' asked Miriam.

'We don't believe in analysts, Miriam,' said Clare. 'Have you forgotten?' and she smiled. Miriam fumed.

She considered the smile uncalled for and somewhat sly. She had known several analysts and spent many a pleasurable fifty minutes or so describing to Clare their various shortcomings, both professional and personal, without realizing the extent to which she was influencing her friend. Standing back and examining her attitude, she saw that while nothing would induce her to subject herself to their ministrations, she yet considered that they might be of some use, when all else failed, in the case of the feeble of intellect, those who had not read some books or been brought up in the same ambience.

'The trouble with you,' said Clare, 'is that you wouldn't let them tinker with your Rolls Royce but you'd let them get at someone else's Morris Minor.'

For the time being Miriam was defeated.

The next morning she heard the cuckoo calling in the valley.

'You don't get cuckoos at this time of year,' said Clare knowledgeably.

'Then this must be one who nobody told,' said Miriam. 'Listen.'

'Probably a wood-pigeon,' said Clare, but Miriam found the voice of only one bird recognizable and she knew a cuckoo when she heard one.

PART TWO

It was five minutes to noon next morning when Eloise came home with the baby. Naturally, they questioned her.

'Where did you get that?' asked Miriam.

'It's mine,' said Eloise.

'Are you out of your mind?' asked her mother.

'It's mine,' said Eloise.

By the time Simon arrived home Clare had drunk half a bottle of vodka and was still sober, Miriam was white-faced and tight-lipped and Eloise had gone to lie down with the baby.

'Simon,' said Miriam, 'something has happened.' Simon, who had been about to ask after the welfare of his cat, thought better of it, especially after he had seen him washing his face in the corner of the kitchen.

'Eloise,' he said, and stared round, looking for her.

'Oh, yes,' said Miriam, 'Eloise.'

'What's happened to her?' he cried, now flushing with apprehension. 'Where has she gone?'

'She's gone to bed,' said Clare and fell silent. Miriam could think of no socially acceptable or emotionally neutral terms in which to convey the intelligence that Eloise had either pilfered a new-born child or somehow contrived to give birth to it in a ditch.

'She's got a baby,' she said.

'Where from?' asked Simon, wrinkling his smooth forehead in incomprehension.

'That's just the point,' said Miriam. 'She says it's hers.'

'She's not pregnant,' said Simon.

'No, she isn't,' said Miriam grimly. 'But was she? That is the question.'

'She always wears those shapeless things,' said Clare, to whom this had so long been a source of grievance. 'How could anyone tell?'

'We must get her to a doctor,' said Miriam.

'No, we must not,' said Clare. They had been arguing for hours about the course they should take. 'What if it's not hers?' she cried for the thousandth time.

'Then we must refer to the proper authorities,' said Miriam, also for the thousandth time.

'If you say that again I'll scream,' said Clare.

'You've been screaming all day,' said Miriam. 'It doesn't help.'

'It helps me,' said Clare sombrely, slumping down in the armchair. Simon was running upstairs. His footsteps seemed to shake the whole house.

'Poor Simon,' said Miriam, moving towards the stove. She trod on the paw of M'sieu who protested loudly. 'Oh, damn,' she said, who never swore.

'I think I'm going mad,' said Clare.

'She has to be examined by a doctor,' said Miriam. 'If she has had a baby she'll need medical attention.'

'What you mean,' said Clare accusingly, 'is that you don't believe she has and you want to rush off and tell the police.'

'What else are we to do?' inquired Miriam. 'Be reasonable.' She refused to take offence at Clare's tone. It would only have complicated things further. It was essential that she remain calm.

'It's got nothing to do with reason,' said Clare. Simon fell downstairs.

'I can't wake her,' he said. 'I'm going for the doctor.'

'No,' said Clare, but he had gone. Clare flew to her daughter's bedside. Eloise was sitting up cradling the baby.

'Simon said you were sleeping,' said Clare.

'I was,' said Eloise, 'but I have to feed it,' she added, looking down at the child. Clare flew downstairs again.

'She's going to feed it,' she said.

'I should hope so,' said Miriam. 'Oh, I see what you mean. Can she?' Clare flew back upstairs.

'Can you?' she asked. Eloise unbuttoned her nightdress and pushed the lace aside. She put the baby to her breast and since it seemed content with the arrangement Clare went downstairs again, slowly this time. 'She can,' she said. 'She must have been pregnant without knowing. It does happen. And she *always* wore those shapeless frocks . . .' It seemed that Eloise's choice of apparel had become the focus of her wrath.

'I need a drink,' said Miriam.

'But how the stupid little article could go so far

without knowing I will never understand,' said her exasperated parent.

'It might not be the right time to remind you,' said Miriam, 'but you too were – to put it mildly – uncertain of your dates.'

'But at least I knew I was pregnant,' said Clare. 'I knew something was going to happen.'

And now relief filled the women and the air of the kitchen, which had felt acid with their anxiety, mellowed and the light softened. They would not be subjected to another investigation by the police and the embarrassment of a trial for kidnapping. Only M'sieu contributed a note of discord. He was restless and jumped from the chair to the table, his eyes wide.

'Bloody cat,' said Clare without animosity. 'I wonder how long it will be before Simon finds a doctor.'

It was not long, for it seemed the doctor had found Simon.

'He was on his way here,' said Simon. 'I met him at the bottom of the lane. He said someone had told him he was needed.'

'Who on earth could it've been?' wondered Clare.

'I have heard,' said Miriam, 'that in all country districts, the local inhabitants know you have a cold before you have uttered your first warning sneezes.'

'All the same . . .' said Clare.

'There are eyes everywhere,' said Simon unexpectedly. 'I've seen absolutely no one round here except the shepherd and the gamekeeper,' said Clare, 'and how would they know?'

'If she had the baby on the hills,' said Simon, 'one of them might have seen her.'

'Then why didn't they bring her home instead of leaving her to come back all on her own?' asked Clare.

'With the baby,' corrected Miriam. 'They might've been too far away, or perhaps a natural delicacy prevented them from intruding.'

'I don't think natural delicacy should come into it in an emergency,' said Clare.

'The whole thing is highly peculiar,' said Miriam, reflecting that of all Eloise's divergencies from the norm this was the most remarkable. 'But all's well that ends well.' Her voice lacked conviction.

Simon also looked unconvinced. He had not smiled once at the news of his fatherhood but appeared anxious and unhappy. Clare glanced at him surreptitiously. She was irritated to find that she felt guilty on her daughter's behalf: ashamed not of but for her. Embarrassed by the fecklessness that could lead a girl to be delivered on a mountainside without preparation or ceremony. There were rules and customs to be observed in the circumstance of birth and Eloise had simply ignored them all. It was thoughtless; it was unseemly, it was unhygienic. She had defied all the ordinances of affection, society and medicine and disregarded all the proprieties. This sudden birth was as disconcerting as sudden death. Murder, thought Clare before she could call her thoughts to order. 'I don't know why we're all so melancholy,' she said, sadly.

The doctor came downstairs. He was a big man but he moved quietly and spoke with a calm voice; his face was expressionless. According to him everything was perfectly normal. He spoke as though English were not his first language and Miriam thought he must be another of the border people and more accustomed to Welsh.

'Shouldn't she have a prescription?' asked Clare. In her experience no doctor departed without leaving a prescription: it put a formal seal on a consultation, tangible evidence that a medical man had done what was expected of him. He paused on his way to the door and turned – it seemed to Miriam reluctantly – and put his case on the table, opening it half-way so that no one could see what lay within. He wrote rapidly on a small sheet of paper and handed it to Clare, who glanced at it and passed it to Simon. 'You can pick it up tomorrow,' she said. The doctor's writing was, as always, illegible to the unprofessional eye. He extended a hand and Miriam, who stood nearest, shook it. It was icily cold. Doctors often had cold hands, she remembered, wincing.

'So that's all right,' she said when he had left. He had said that the nurse would call tomorrow but there was nothing to worry about, nothing at all.

'He was awfully large for a doctor,' said Clare into the sudden silence. 'Doctors tend to be much the same size. I don't know if you noticed. You seldom come across such an enormous one.'

'You're jabbering, Clare,' said Miriam, and silence fell again. Miriam could think of nothing more to say. But too much was being left unsaid. She knew with a worrying certainty that none of them knew what to do next. Knew that they shared a surely unnatural disinclination to look at Eloise's baby. Knew that one of them must soon do something to disrupt this eerie passivity, to shake off the heavy torpor and return to life or . . .

It was Simon who broke the spell. He said loudly that surely Eloise should have something to eat and he went upstairs. When he came down he said that she had requested beef tea and a bowl of gruel. Of the baby he did not speak and Miriam, for some reason obscure even to herself, thought of Wittgenstein.

'Oh God,' said Clare. 'We haven't got so much as an Oxo cube and I don't know what gruel is.'

'I'll make her some porridge,' said Miriam. Her mouth was dry and she felt a little deaf. 'Can we see the baby now?' she asked, and it took a great effort to say it.

Clare started as though she had forgotten there was a baby. She had seen only the back of its head. It had silvery hair. 'I'll go and get it,' she cried on a high, gay note that failed to convince.

'I'll come with you,' said Miriam, 'and look at Eloise.'

Eloise had fallen asleep again, her black hair spread on the pillow. Miriam stooped to look at her face. Something like a fine, broken veil lay across her eyes, barely perceptible except where the lamplight glinted on its strands. Clare was lifting the child from the crook of her daughter's arm and while she was engrossed in half-remembered care for the lolling head, the soft spine, Miriam ran her fingers across its mother's face. The web clung to them and she almost cried out, brushing her hand violently against the rough wool of her skirt.

'Oh look,' said Clare, gazing down at the baby. 'Isn't it sweet? Just look at its eyes.'

The baby looked up at them – a pale, pale face and eyes as green as young willow leaves reflected in lake water, and its silvery, silvery hair.

'Sweet,' agreed Miriam and it was all she would say.

Eloise was up with the birds the next morning while the rest of them slept. She carried a carved wooden cradle into the garden and laid her baby in it, lapped in white linen. She gazed down at its face as she might have gazed down at a pool to see the ripples drift across the surface, changing with every movement of the breeze. A bird sang from a tree deep in the woods, a high, clear song, and the baby listened. Eloise wanted to sing her own song but she waited. Perhaps it was best not to interrupt the accord of bird and child in the still morning.

Clare woke as the sun climbed higher, exclaimed in guilty horror at the lateness of the hour, although it was far earlier than her usual rising time, rose and went straight to Eloise's room. Miriam was awakened by a shout.

'What are you doing?' she demanded, emerging from her room and bumping into Clare on the landing. 'Who was yelling?'

'I was calling you,' said Clare. 'Eloise has gone with the baby.'

'She's probably downstairs,' said Miriam, consulting her watch. 'It's late.'

'But she shouldn't be up,' said Clare, starting down the stairs. The parlour door was open and she glanced in. Simon had gone to sleep on the sofa but he wasn't there now. The kitchen too was empty. 'Ohhh,' said Clare.

'Eloise is in the garden,' said Miriam, indicating the window and re-tying the sash of her dressing-gown. She went to put the kettle on in a prosaic, matter-of-fact sort of way, as one who is not perturbed by curious, even inexplicable events; but who continues to shoulder the mundane burdens of life without remark. She felt it would be more necessary than ever, in the immediate future, for someone to behave like this. Clare was now visible through the window, expostulating with her daughter on the lawn.

'What are you doing out of bed?' she was inquiring. 'And why have you brought the baby out? It'll catch its death of cold.'

'It's a lovely day,' said Eloise, 'and I don't need to lie in.'

'Wait till the nurse gets here,' threatened Clare. Miriam watched, idly drying a mug and wondering at the tendency of even the most unlikely women to carry on like the mother in Jack and the Beanstalk when the urge came over them. Or maybe grandmotherhood had imbued Clare with a sense of deep responsibility. 'About time,' muttered Miriam, knowing she was being unfair but too exhausted by the tumults of yesterday to be meticulous in her judgements. She made a pot of strong tea and boiled three eggs.

'She won't come in,' said Clare, coming in herself and sitting down.

'I suppose she knows what she wants to do,' said Miriam, 'and it's quite warm today.'

'She shouldn't be up,' repeated Clare. 'It's only the second day.' Miriam poured her a cup of tea.

'I believe,' she said, 'that state-of-the-art medical opinion now holds that it is preferable to leap out of bed and rush round before the stitches are dry. This, of course, is in the case of an operation, but I am told that the same advice is offered to the recently delivered. It prevents clots forming in the arteries. I suppose that all that bouncing about doesn't give them time to develop.'

'Don't be disgusting,' said Clare. 'Show some sympathy.' Miriam asked herself to whom Clare wished her to exhibit this soothing quality but said nothing. She intended to have a quiet and restful day.

The nurse arrived.

'Perhaps you'll tell her she shouldn't be up,' said Clare. 'She could get a chill out there.' The nurse was businesslike. She went into the garden, spoke briskly to

Eloise, looked briskly at the baby and then sat briskly down on a garden chair.

'What do you suppose she's saying?' asked Clare fretfully.

'She's probably asking pertinent fleshly questions about bowels and bosoms and things. Birth isn't just about champagne and cigars and layettes, you know.'

'I wonder if I should tell her that Eloise was premature?' suggested Clare. 'It might run in the family.'

'She wasn't premature,' said Miriam. 'You just can't count.' But Clare was determined to join the group on the lawn.

'I'll see if she wants a cup of tea,' she announced decisively and went out. She hadn't even put on her make-up, noted Miriam. It was seldom that Clare presented a naked face to the world. Miriam went to her room to get dressed.

'Where did you get that?' asked Clare, eyeing the cradle with disfavour. It was undoubtedly what people described as antique: a dark wood carved with leaves and flowers, but Clare suspected it of being insanitary. She treasured her own antiques, but she wouldn't have eaten off one unless she knew it had been disinfected. The cradle made her think of ancient plagues and afflictions, of coffins.

'The attic,' said the nurse, who was tilting the baby's chin to look into its eyes – its willow-green eyes. Clare opened her mouth and shut it again. Eloise must have disclosed its provenance and it would be unwise to antagonize a nurse by saying that you hadn't been speaking to her.

'I'll get you a nice new one,' she said. No one responded to this offer and Clare felt that they were scarcely aware of her presence. 'A nice, clean white one from Harrods,' she said to impress the nurse; not only with her sensible intention, but her generosity, her status. Let no one suppose that Eloise was just another ordinary, unmarried mother. They ignored her. The nurse as unmoved as though she had never heard of Harrods. Clare now noticed that, under the white linen sheet, the cradle was lined with rushes, still green and flowering. Since she had already indicated her disapproval of the cradle it was impossible to protest further without sounding like a carping, scolding mother. She wasn't wanted here. She went into the kitchen and wept.

'I think you're having a sort of belated couvade,' said Miriam, not unsympathetically. 'A kind of projected post-parturition depression.' Clare sniffed. It was cheering to have her discomfort recognized, but it should have been the nurse who had noticed. Should have been the nurse saying, 'You don't look too bright. This must all have been a great shock to you. Take this tonic.' Nurses were not what they were. Reflecting on this and the general unsatisfactory state of the health services, she began to think in more detail about the nurse: there were several criticisms that Clare felt could justly be levelled at her.

'She hasn't examined Eloise,' she began.

'There is a policy known as minimal interference,' said Miriam. 'During the last century there was a doctor who noticed that those wounded soldiers who were somehow overlooked by the surgeons tended to recover from their injuries. Others were not so lucky.'

'Surgeons didn't wash their hands in those days,' said Clare. 'She hasn't examined the baby either.'

'She's looking at it now,' said Miriam.

'Not properly,' said Clare. 'She looks like a bloke,' she added.

'Nurses often have a tendency towards a certain manliness,' said Miriam. 'Particularly senior nurses. It may have something to do with the change in the uniform.'

'And she's got the most huge teeth,' said Clare disconsolately.

'Perhaps they're false,' said Miriam. She had begun excusing the nurse's apparent deficiencies merely to reassure Clare and was irritated to find herself in the notoriously suspect position of defence counsel.

'Why are you sticking up for her?' inquired Clare. 'It isn't like you.'

'I'm trying to take a sensible, reasonable view,' said Miriam.

'You're trying not to worry me,' said Clare, 'and it doesn't help. If we were at sea and the boat had a hole in it, you'd be saying it was only a little one instead of trying to caulk it.' Her friend's unexpected percipience left Miriam momentarily at a loss. 'You don't usually go round saying everything in the garden's lovely,' complained Clare. 'I don't know what's come over you.'

Involuntarily Miriam looked out of the window to study the garden. Eloise was leaning against the apple tree that held the mistletoe and the baby was at her breast. Such an idyllic scene should surely not have assaulted her senses with a desolate impression of parasitism; of an ancient, wordless evil that need not rely on humanity for expression but persisted in corruption. For an instant nothing out there was lovely.

'I'll call her in,' said Miriam, moving, too quickly, towards the door. As she trod the soft grass and smelled the flowered air she found them hateful. The beaming heartsease, the bland mallow, the confidentially nodding roses mocked her misgivings. As she moved nearer to the three under the trees she saw that the woods had moved closer. Behind her, she knew, the ivy had clung more tightly to the red house, its blind tendrils seeking out the interstices of brick, the imperceptible gap between window and wall, the weakness of structure: indifferent, implacable, hungry. Accursed nature, she thought lest her command of language, blessed words, should leave her. But when she spoke she found her words foolish, the gibberish of a trained animal. 'Time for lunch. She must keep her strength up mustn't she, Nurse? No sense in neglecting her meals. She's eating for two now. Time the baby had its nap. And Eloise must rest mustn't she, Nurse . . .'

Nurse slowly turned her attention to the interloper,

wearing a look of polite resignation as of one accustomed to the clumsy interference of the uninitiated. 'She must be quiet,' she said. 'No people except . . .'

'Except who?' asked Miriam as Nurse hesitated.

'Two of us will call,' said Nurse, 'two . . .'

'Social workers,' said Miriam, suddenly back to earth. 'You're sending social workers round.'

'That's right,' said Nurse smoothly, 'social workers.'

Eloise got to her feet and put the baby in its cradle. 'I'm hungry,' she said. Miriam stood and watched the nurse leave. She had an impression that, had she been unobserved, she would not have taken the path to the lane but have moved easily and silently into the woods. Eloise followed Miriam into the kitchen.

'Aren't you bringing the baby in?' asked Clare.

'It likes it out there,' said Eloise.

'She isn't English is she, that nurse?' said Clare.

'I don't know,' said Eloise. Clare, who had been about to say more, turned instead to the cupboard.

'I'll have one as well,' said Miriam, knowing that Clare was reaching for the vodka. She also thought she knew what Clare had left unsaid. It would have been something to the effect that the nurse had struck her as hardly human. Miriam felt it too.

Simon was late coming home. 'Where did he go?' asked Clare.

'Work, I expect,' said Eloise.

'It's a funny day to go to work,' said her mother

149

disagreeably, 'when he's just had his first child. I never heard anything like it.'

'He probably thought he'd be in the way,' said Miriam, hastily pacific. 'Max was much the same when Eloise arrived.'

'Simon doesn't like babies,' said Eloise.

'Nonsense,' said Clare, as there seemed no other proper response. She was baffled by her daughter's detachment and now felt it incumbent on herself to stand up for Simon. 'He had to go to the chemist,' she remembered.

When he did arrive he was not the same, nice normal boy of whom Miriam approved. He was silent and emanated an air of dull, dumb misery, very trying on those in his vicinity.

'*Men*,' said Clare under her breath in the age-old way of women. 'Did you get the prescription?' she demanded. Still silent, Simon produced a packet of aspirin from his pocket.

'Is that it?' said Clare, astonished and aggrieved. 'We could have got that without a prescription. More cheaply,' she added.

Simon said nothing. He had gone, as bidden, to the chemist in the market town and felt in his breast pocket for the prescription. There had been nothing there but his pen and a dry, faded leaf. He knew he hadn't lost it and that was when the sadness had seized him, eliminating thought, defying him to speculate. He had bought the packet of aspirin and spent the rest of the day walking the few streets, retracing his steps again and again, so that those who saw him thought him one of those unfortunates, released into the community, and avoided him.

'Simon,' said Miriam, 'what are these scratches on your arms?'

'They're nothing much,' said Simon indifferently, glancing at them. 'The hedge needs cutting back. It's almost closed the lane. I had to fight through the brambles.'

'It was all right yesterday,' said Miriam.

'Things grow quickly here,' said Simon. 'They grow out of control.'

'Where's M'sieu?' he said. They had all forgotten about M'sieu. He hadn't even had his fish.

'He'll be sleeping on someone's bed,' said Clare. 'You'd better be careful he doesn't sleep on the baby's face.'

'M'sieu,' called Simon, 'M'sieu.'

'Miriam,' said Clare, 'we'll have to go shopping to-morrow. We need milk and bread and disposable nappies and baby oil and vegetables and meat.'

Simon ignored the intended rebuke, seeming not even to notice it. He went to look for his straying cat and found him at last under Miriam's bed. 'Naughty,' said Simon fondly and rubbed his face in M'sieu's fur. 'Miaou,' said M'sieu piteously.

'There's meat in the hills,' said Eloise, who had flatly refused to stay in bed.

'I don't suggest we go poaching,' said Miriam on the spur of the moment, for she had heard something unpleasant in these words from the petal lips of the fastidious Eloise, who had campaigned to save veal calves. 'The gamekeeper wouldn't like it at all. He would shoot us without compunction.'

'I thought he was a friend of yours,' said Clare, who had also shrunk at her daughter's choice of words and was relieved to have the conversation shifted to another line, no matter how parallel.

'Even if he didn't shoot us,' said Miriam, 'it could only lead to unpleasantness. One has to be so careful in a rural district.'

Clare considered. 'I'm sick of rural,' she said at last. 'I think it's time we went back to town.'

Simon surprised them. 'No,' he said violently. M'sieu leapt from his lap.

'I mean all of us,' explained Clare. 'I mean I meant Eloise and the baby too. We can look after them better in town.'

Simon seemed to relax, his muscles visibly untensing. Many young fathers, Miriam told herself, preferred to have older, experienced women in the house when it contained a new baby. M'sieu crept back.

'No,' said Eloise.

'Yes,' said Simon.

The evening ended in wasted argument and Clare wept again.

*

In the night she went to Miriam's room and shook her awake. 'I can't sleep,' she said. 'Let's go down and make a pot of tea.' Miriam thought it easier not to protest. 'It always makes me think of Christmas, drinking tea in the dark in the early morning,' said Clare. Miriam looked at her watch. 'You know what I mean,' insisted Clare.

'No, I don't,' said Miriam factually.

'There's something wrong,' said Clare. Miriam, despite the strange circumstances which had brought her to this realization, was relieved both by the fact that her friend appreciated this and that she had the new-found courage to say so. In the past Clare had frequently refused to admit to matters which might cause her consternation. Now she appeared admirably calm. 'Simon's still sleeping in the parlour,' she said.

'That's probably quite wise,' said Miriam. 'He has to go to work and the baby would only keep him awake.' Then she stopped speaking for, now she thought of it, she had not once heard the baby cry.

'He hasn't picked it up or looked at it at all,' said Clare. 'We've all been too busy to notice but it is so.' It didn't seem to Miriam like a proper time to ask what Clare had been so busy about.

She cast around for the appropriate psychological jargon which might serve to silence her friend's fears. 'He hasn't had time to bond with it,' she offered at last without conviction.

'Oh nuts,' said Clare and Miriam could not demur.

'Nevertheless,' she said, 'it is true that men do not feel the same way about babies as women do. They never have.'

'I know that,' said Clare impatiently. 'I haven't fallen for all that New Man talk. But he's *unhappy*.'

'Eloise isn't,' observed Miriam.

'She soon will be,' said Clare, 'if Simon is.'

Miriam pondered. 'You don't want her to leave Simon, do you?' she asked.

'No,' said Clare.

'Is it,' suggested Miriam carefully, 'that if she leaves Simon she'll come and live with you?'

'There is that,' agreed Clare candidly, 'but that isn't really it.' She hesitated. She wanted to explain that she wished Eloise to have a normal, boring life and if she left her child's father then it would inevitably be eventful. Probably just as boring in the end, but not in the peaceful fashion that would allow her to grow old without scalding regret. 'I don't want her to be like me,' she concluded and closed her lips defiantly.

'Oh, Clare,' said Miriam.

'I don't want pity,' said Clare. 'I have no regrets . . .'

'You lie,' interrupted Miriam.

'You're cruel,' said Clare.

'No pity,' Miriam reminded her.

'Well anyway, I just don't want her ending up on her own with Clauds round every corner. I'm old-fashioned.' Clare spread her hands in a submissive gesture. Miriam found her admission disarming but they had still not touched on the heart of the matter. The old question of the *oddness* of Eloise.

'Is she mad?' asked Clare, as aware as Miriam of what had not been addressed.

'I don't think so,' said Miriam.

'Drugs?' said Clare.

'I don't know,' said Miriam. Since she had entertained doubts about her own sanity, she did not presently feel qualified to pontificate too earnestly on the subject. 'This is a weird place,' she said, not to displace responsibility for her own seemingly disordered mental condition, but because it was time to bring fear into the open.

'I know,' said Clare. 'Don't think I haven't noticed.'

Miriam bowed her head.

'This place is too far from the shops,' said Clare in the morning light. She elaborated lest they should think she meant Fortnum & Mason or Harvey Nichols. 'You could run out of supplies and have no way of getting any. Nappies and baby food and salt and pepper. You can't expect Simon to spend his life running backwards and forwards because the cupboard is bare.' She felt that she and Simon had now made common cause. Eloise took no notice of her. 'Drains,' continued Clare. 'I really do not trust the drains here. There's a very peculiar smell in the sink. I'm certain it's not safe to drink the water from the stream. And the rapist,' she went on for good measure, 'they haven't caught the rapist.'

She was doing it again, thought Miriam, over-egging the pudding. Eloise was still unmoved, but sat placidly chewing bacon rind.

'What would Moonbird say if she could see you doing that?' asked Clare – ill-advisedly in Miriam's opinion. But Eloise made no response. 'I asked you a question,' insisted Clare. Her wakeful night had apparently improved neither her disposition nor her capacity for tact. Miriam sighed. 'What would Moonbird say?' repeated Clare.

'Who?' said Eloise dreamily. She had put her baby out under the trees and her thoughts were with it. She was lost in contemplation of its lake-green eyes, its silken silver hair. Nothing else was real to her. There was nothing else.

Clare, under the influence of encroaching panic, wanted to shake her, to slap her, to bring her back . . . 'We're leaving here tomorrow,' she said. 'The baby must have proper medical attention. It can't stay here with just those foreign fools who don't know anything. I don't care what you say. We're going.'

'I'm not,' said Eloise. 'I can't.'

'What do you mean – you can't?' said her mother.

'The rain,' said Eloise, 'the river.' It was a fine clear day with a few high, white clouds, soft as babies' blankets, scarcely moving in the heavens.

'You'll see,' said Clare. 'Just you wait. I've made up my mind. If you're going to be difficult I'll tell your father to cut off your allowance. Then what will you do?'

Miriam got up. 'What you need,' she said, 'is a breath of fresh air. We'll go for a walk.'

'I don't want to go for a walk,' said Clare. 'What's the point of a bloody walk if there aren't any shops?'

It seemed inevitable that they should climb the hillside to the place which had been arranged by the hand of a Master and where the water fell to the pool in the hollow. There were small, unshod hoof marks in the dried mud of the lane and a multitude of flies.

'I hate flies,' said Clare as though she were unique in this prejudice.

Miriam half expected her to demand that they turn back, but Clare strode doggedly on, panting a little as the gradient rose. 'Ahh,' she breathed as they reached their destination and she sat down on the grass.

Miriam could not forbid her, could not say that she feared she was committing a profanity. It was as though Clare had carelessly seated herself in the lap of some sleeping beauty: for the dell with its change of scene from the woods below and the moorland above made Miriam think of a princess imprisoned for her worth by those who valued it over the need of recognition or acclaim; who had hidden her from mortal sight behind a bastion of grim forest and laid waste the territory beyond, where the unwary might meet death in the sudden mists and unmarked precipices.

'I'm starving after that route march,' said Clare. 'I

wish we'd brought sandwiches.' Miriam imagined beer cans and polythene containers littering the grass under the dappling shadows. It was, she supposed, eventually inevitable. As the human race proliferated, breeding generation after generation of tourists, it would probe into every secret corner of what Moonbird and the optimistic referred to as Mother Earth. She could not know that this was what the watchers dreaded too, dreaded above all things, but she had never been so aware of being alien and she knew with bleak certainty that the earth cared nothing for humanity.

'Perfect spot for a picnic,' pronounced Clare. 'I bet Moonbird would love it here,' she said after a while. 'I can just see her prancing round in circles with a bagful of hard-boiled eggs and a ball of wool and a pile of vegetation stuck in her hair.'

'Is that what she does?' asked Miriam, despite herself. 'I thought she mostly sat in darkened rooms swinging crystals and burning incense and messing about with tarot cards.'

'She does that too,' said Clare, 'and rain dances. I try not to think about it.' A breeze sprang from nowhere, stirring the still leaves, and with it came the stench of decay.

'There's something dead,' said Miriam.

'How foul,' said Clare. She got up and looked round. 'It's probably a sheep drowned in the stream and we've been drinking the water.' She set off in search of the source of the smell and further evidence that the country was an unsuitable, insanitary place to keep a new-born baby.

'Leave it, Clare,' called Miriam. 'It'll be horrible.' Clare didn't hear her. Her ears were full of the sound of water and she was scrambling down the steep bank where it fell. Miriam followed her reluctantly, remembering that in her youth Clare had been as impetuous as her daughter now was, and still manifested this tiresome quality at inconvenient moments. 'You'll break your neck,' she shouted, sliding down a stony slope.

Clare was standing on a flat rock looking at the thing that lay beside the water. Miriam joined her.

'He's half devoured,' said Clare. 'Something's been eating him.'

For a moment Miriam saw only darkness broken by small stars. She wished Clare would do something instead of standing there looking thoughtful. Somebody should scream. It was expected. If an unburied body lay rotting in the daylight then screaming ensued.

'Are you all right?' Clare was asking. 'Come away and sit down.' It was all wrong, thought Miriam. It was Clare who should be in shock, but Clare was as calm as an undertaker going about his trade out of the public gaze. Shock, she told herself, could take many forms. It had grown impossibly cold.

They met the shepherd at the head of the lane: he was leaning against the stile looking out over the valley, his dog lying at his feet. It growled at them and its master pushed it with his foot, silencing it. They told him what they'd seen.

'I believe,' said Miriam, clearly, 'that we just caught up with the sex-offender.'

The shepherd said it was probably an old sheep and Miriam said, no, it had been a man. Clare said nothing. The shepherd said he'd go and have a look and Miriam said she'd show him the place. Clare said it was just by the waterfall and he couldn't miss it. The shepherd said he knew the place. Miriam fell silent.

They said nothing of their discovery to Eloise and Clare made Miriam a cup of hot, sweet tea.

In what seemed a very short time the shepherd accompanied by his hostile dog appeared at the kitchen door. He said it was just as he'd thought – only an old dead sheep, a skull and a few ribs and a sodden fleece. He gave them a whitened bone as evidence and left, whistling.

'What did he say?' asked Clare. 'You understand them.'

'He said it was only an old sheep,' said Miriam, 'and we'd be silly to tell the police.'

'Country people,' said Clare. 'They don't like the police. I expect they're right.' The visual memory of what had once been a man was already fading and she was quite prepared to accept that, in this instance, she had made a mistake. A calculated admission of error was sometimes advisable. A police investigation would undoubtedly delay their departure. All she had seen was an old dead sheep. The shepherd had said so and he should know. 'Anyway, we're going soon. Look, it's started to rain again.'

All night Miriam lay and listened to the rain. When she closed her eyes she saw the horror that lay by the stream. When she opened them she saw nothing, for the window was as blank as though it were blinded. No moon, no stars: nothing but the rain and darkness and the strange cold. She reached out to switch on her bedside lamp but there was no responding surge of light. There is a power cut, she thought in so many words. The rain has brought the lines down. The light has gone from the earth, said her undisciplined mind. It is a power failure, her reason contradicted. A failure of *electrical* power, she amended, lest her fearful self should collude with the forces of evil and cause her to submit to terror. There are candles by the kitchen door, she told her other self, and a box of matches lies beside them. When the sensible woman cannot sleep and is troubled by hypnogogic images she goes in search of material things, a source of light, an extra blanket. She reads a carefully chosen book to take her mind off things unholy. What she does not do, she thought, in a case like this, is count sheep.

Miriam climbed carefully out of bed and made her way to the door, using her memory to guide her across the few feet of floor that separated her from access to the stairs. Surely in so small a house she could feel her way to the kitchen. The darkness was absolute but she kept her eyes wide open as though in denial: to close them would have been to admit to impotence, to allow the night its triumph. When she walked into the wall, for a horrifying moment, she had the impression that the wall had moved forward to bar her way. She had been moving slowly in an elderly shuffle, her hands before her, and now she stood with her forehead against the implacable wall with no palpable sign within her reach that it was interrupted anywhere by a means of escape. The grave has no doors, she thought. Gehenna has no doors. Pull yourself together, Miriam. She began to move sideways, touching the wall with fingertips and flattened palms, uncertain now whether she regarded it as gaoler or guide, but loth to part with it in case there was nothing else. When her thigh bumped into what must be the bed she felt for the pillow, the turned-back sheet and realized that she stood at its foot and was totally disoriented. Without troubling to fumble her way to the head, she pulled back the sheet and got into bed. Doubtless the dawn would come eventually and she would then revise her knowledge of the relative positions of door and window and the distribution of furniture. There was nothing to fear, she told her shivering self.

She woke to a sullen grey light, wondering where she was, since she lay facing the door and not the window and had no pillow under her head. She was as comforted by the return of day as a lost child sighting its mother, no matter how ill was her mood. The rain had lessened but not ceased. Miriam rearranged her bedclothes in the proper order and got dressed. She preferred not to speculate on how she had managed to traverse the room in the night without encountering obstacles: the chest of drawers, the chair, the window frame. It didn't matter now nor ever would – unless there were a next time. But she did wonder why she had been forbidden to walk in the night and what Eloise had been doing.

Eloise was in the kitchen, rinsing plates with her left hand while she held the baby with her right. It peered over her shoulder at Miriam with its ice-green eyes and she thought she had never seen so self-possessed an infant. It would have been impertinent to say things to it – cootchy-coo or diddums or any of the other idiocies with which it was customary to address the recently born. It looked as though it knew too much and would have found it futile to attempt to communicate with others. Miriam considered it lacking in charm. She was surprised later in the morning when Clare exclaimed over its air of enchantment, crying that it had obviously been here before. Miriam could not count the times she had heard women say this. Previously it had merely sounded silly. Now Clare's remark made her ill at ease, as though a novice had suddenly sounded a true note on a difficult instrument.

Simon didn't like the baby much either. He said very little but it was obvious to Miriam. He scarcely ever looked at it, but went to work as soon as he rose and to bed straight after his supper. Clare appeared to regard this as perfectly normal, which in a way, supposed Miriam, it was. Men were unnecessary during, and for some time after, a confinement. The sexes were in rare agreement on this, although it had been lately fashionable in liberal circles to pretend otherwise. There was talk of a sharing of labour, but the men who endeavoured to concur in this idea were usually the ones with whiskers and woolly hats who carried the baby about in a knapsack, and the notion was dying a natural death. Nor did M'sieu like the baby. Clare had been deeply concerned lest the cat should choose to sleep in the cradle on the baby's face and suffocate it, but wherever the baby was, M'sieu was not – he never came within feet of it.

Eloise had now taken over the parlour as a microcosmic world for the baby and herself, leaving Simon alone in their bedroom. She had spread the old, unyielding sofa with white lawn and lace and put the cradle beside it, and she had hung trails of ivy and mistletoe from the picture rails. Clare had said in an aside to Miriam that it looked as though Eloise thought Christmas had come. Miriam had pondered the implications of this remark, which had clearly escaped her friend, but had said only that the garlands of mistletoe and ivy predated Christmas by some considerable time. There were jugs containing meadowsweet and broom and ungainly twigs of oak and yew on the window-sill and the table top of Benares brass, and all in all, the room with its green scents overpowering the old smell of ancient perfume and mildew was redolent of the forest. Moonbird, thought Miriam, would doubtless find it delightful but it made her uneasy. Clare's disapproval still focused on the cradle in the carving of which, at the foot, she insisted she had discerned a nasty face, all covered in leaves. She would have preferred her daughter to be surrounded by roses, carnations and gypsophila at such a time and still yearned to see the child in a bassinet, but there was really very little she could do about it as long as they remained in the red house. She returned to the subject of departure as soon as Simon had left for work.

'Until you find a place of your own,' she said coaxingly to her daughter, 'you and Simon and the baby can stay in the flat and I'll stay with Miriam until you find somewhere.' Miriam raised her eyebrows. Clare obviously considered herself to be making a great sacrifice with this suggestion.

'Now wait a minute . . .' Miriam was beginning, about to construct a sentence which, while consonant with amity, would yet preclude an extended visit from her friend, when there was a knock at the front door.

'Who's that?' demanded Clare as they heard the door open. She knew she had locked it the previous night and Simon had left by the kitchen door. There was no time, and in the event, there seemed no real reason to protest as two women entered the kitchen. They had come, they said in concert, from the Social Services.

'Good,' said Clare, sounding to Miriam, who had had dealings with social workers, premature if not overly optimistic. 'You can explain to her how much better the baby would be in town with all the proper facilities – clean water and shops and the park.' Miriam sighed again. Even she was surprised at the lack of thought behind this plea. It was possible that social workers would prefer people to live in towns but it was not inevitable. They might answer, with justification, that town water was reliable neither in quality nor the aggravated matter of supply, that the air in towns was dangerously polluted, the parks floored with dog excreta, and a refuge for people injudiciously turned out of secure accommodation. There was much to be said in favour of the country and, as Miriam had expected, they said it. Clare grew increasingly indignant but held her tongue until they had gone, whereupon she became rather grand.

'Who did they think they were talking to?' she inquired. 'Who do they think they are? Did they hint they could take the baby away or was I imagining it?'

'You have to be very careful with them,' said Miriam. 'They do have terrible powers. They can take a child away without so much as a by-your-leave.' There had been several well-publicized cases in the recent past where the Social Services had indeed exerted their rights in this fashion.

'We're living in a police state,' said Clare. 'I'll speak to Ralph about it.' Ralph was her MP, but whether he was a servant of the state or a representative of the people she was not sure, so changed course. 'They may not have been social workers,' she said. 'You're always hearing stories about funny-looking women turning up at people's doors, demanding to examine the baby or trying to take it away. Mind you . . .' she added, 'social workers mostly look funny too. It must be awfully hard to tell a real one from a pretending one. Those two could've been either. They were obviously lesbians but then so are loads of social workers.' She paused. 'But they had those funny foreign voices too,' she went on, 'and they didn't sound properly official somehow. More as though they'd learned a bit of the jargon but didn't know quite how to use it.' Miriam thought this perceptive: she had had the same impression. Now did not seem the time to expand on it. She had been a little afraid, and repelled by the masculine air of the social workers who had been identically dressed and often spoken simultaneously. There was too much unbridled emotion in the house, and an admission of timorousness would not come well from her. She feared that much could be lost were she now to appear unreliable. It was still raining and the clothes of the social workers had been quite dry. They must have had umbrellas, Miriam had told herself emphatically.

'Don't worry,' she said bravely. 'I've dealt with their sort before.' The lane became a torrent but Miriam refused to think about it. Once, over the drumming of the rain, she thought she heard a great splashing as though some swift beast were passing by.

*

In the morning the rain had stopped and a tentative sunlight illumined the garden. Clare looked out of the window and remarked on the undisciplined ways of Welsh weather. 'We could take the baby for a walk,' she said, 'only there's no use in buying a pram before we go because we couldn't push it up that blasted flooded lane with its pits and pot-holes.' She turned to Eloise. 'So that's settled,' she said. 'We'll all go back to town and Simon can follow when we've found you a nice place to live.' Bit rough on Simon, thought Miriam, but she held her tongue.

It was noon when the baby began to cry. Miriam was astonished, not because it was crying so, but because it never had before, not in all its little life.

Clare picked it up and it cried harder. It howled as though in rage, and when Miriam was moved to look at it, she saw not a tear in its sea-green eyes. She had heard old women say of infants who cried for no apparent reason that they were being naughty. In the past she had scorned such absurdity but now she began to wonder. She looked at its furious face and it glared back at her.

Eloise took it from her mother and sang to it. It yelled.

Clare took it back and jiggled it. It shrieked. She handed it to Miriam with a gesture that could not be denied unless she let it drop to the slate floor. It was silent for a moment looking up at her, and then it bellowed.

A row developed. Clare said that this was a clear indication of the necessity of returning to town and Eloise said she could go if she liked. Clare, in stately mode, said she wouldn't dream of leaving a child in such distress. Eloise said it had never bothered her when she herself was little. Clare said she was an ungrateful little bitch and Miriam, who usually held aloof from these scenes, was forced to protest. Clare, although never an ideal, had never been a really neglectful mother. Clare had a glass of vodka.

The baby was silent while the shouting lasted but filled the brief silence by screaming again. Eloise took it into the garden and the uncertain light and laid it down on the grass.

'It'll catch its death of cold,' shouted her mother. 'Stupid girl,' she added *sotto voce*.

'You have to make allowances,' argued Miriam, though not pacifically.

She was haunted this noon by the things of the night. The light was as untrue as poisoned water, bitter and clouded, and there was nothing in which to trust. Distances deceptive, heights and depths as meaningless as though the dark prevailed and all the verdant growth nothing but greedy – for her bones and her flesh and her blood and for her. Miriam, fearing an attack of madness, told herself that she was not the woman to be intimidated by a few buttercups and was far from reassured; for even by the momentary admission of this foolishness it gained power, forcing her to consider its connotations. Flowers throve on death, relying on dissolution for their nourishment, and all the garden was composed of death. She could smell decay on the summer air, on her own familiar breath. If, as Moonbird held, the earth was our mother, then all mankind was an abortion, unwanted. The hell with Moonbird, thought Miriam vigorously. She shook her head, scowling at the prettiness that fringed the great shadow, the horror of chaos that lay just beyond the garlanded hedge and the limits of her comprehension, yet confined by the arc of her brows and the microcosm of her brain. For the first time in her life she was assailed by the fear that she might lose her self-control. The noonday sun seemed simultaneously to grow huger and to disappear.

When night came it came in cold as though it had returned from far away bearing frost on its mantle. The ivy, wind-driven, knocked at the panes like a child egged on to mischief. It was undeniable that the sound could be mistaken for the tap of bony fingers. Miriam wondered if the women who had previously lived in the red house had thought so too. She considered it probable. There were few new perceptions and no new fears. Fear was as old and deadly as man and existed independently, a lieutenant of evil as potent and all-pervasive as lust or anger, searching like disease for a host, for some weakness where it might infiltrate and thrive. Now it seemed to Miriam suddenly female, like a widow greedy for another life.

'There is a touch of autumn in the air,' she said, but the wind howled in the chimney and the baby howled in its cradle and no one heard her. 'Autumn approaches with its Midas touch,' she added, rather in the spirit of one who dresses for dinner, alone in the jungle. No matter what the circumstances, certain proprieties must be observed and it was normal to make conversation when there were several people present. Noise was deleterious not only to the nervous system but to the character, she reflected. She was beginning to hate the baby.

'What?' said Clare fretfully. 'Did you say something?' She wanted to lie down and hide her head under a pillow but there was no escape from this terrible little house and the screams of the outraged creature who dominated it. There was no point in picking it up for it only cried louder. Even Simon had attempted to quieten it, rocking the cradle and saying 'Ssshh', but it had threatened to go into convulsions. Eloise seemed strangely unperturbed, but sat sewing.

'Can't you do anything with it?' asked Clare piteously. 'Isn't there something you can give it? What do they give babies these days?'

'Not laudanum,' said Eloise. Clare ignored this.

'Can't you make it one of your tisanes or something?' she suggested. She was beginning to consider it not so enchanting.

'I might later,' said Eloise calmly and she went on sewing.

In the end they crept, exhausted, to bed, leaving Eloise alone in the parlour with her howling, howling child.

Miriam had alarmed herself with her realization of the sentiment she entertained towards the baby. She considered her feelings unkind, and worse, irrational. Clare and Simon were haggard with weariness and Eloise, although serene, was developing a transparent look. She needed no encouragement to eat meat, red and sanguine, iron-rich liver and protein-laden steaks, but looked more ethereal than when she had confined her diet to greenstuff and beans.

'What you all need,' said Miriam in the morning, 'is a break.' She would herself have been impressed with the nobility of the offer she was about to make if she had not known that her motive was not unselfish. She had to keep irrationality at bay or come to terms with being the kind of person she disapproved of. It was worth making the effort to avoid this. 'Tonight,' she said, 'I want you all to go out to dinner and I shall look after the baby.'

'I don't want to,' said Eloise. There are few things more exasperating than a downright refusal of a magnanimous offer but Miriam remained firm.

'I thought you could go to the steak house,' she said cunningly. One of the stately homes housed in its grounds a franchised branch of this popular enterprise. Eloise hesitated.

'Oh, do let's,' cried Clare with not altogether spurious

enthusiasm. She was not overwhelmed with pleasure at the prospect of an evening with her daughter and Simon in a steak house, but it would be a great relief to get away for a while from the red house and the howls. Besides, she thought it nice of Miriam.

'I insist,' said Miriam. 'M'sieu and I will mind the baby.' The cat, who was washing his face, stopped and blinked at her. 'You can take as long as you like,' went on Miriam courageously.

The baby had stopped screaming but was humming to itself. It fell silent when Miriam pushed open the parlour door, and looked up at her. 'You and me baby,' she said grimly. 'Just you and me.' And she thought it smiled.

She was very thoughtful as she went for her daily constitutional down the lane. The torrent had drained away leaving only shallow mud and the weather seemed quite ordinary today. Neither too bright nor too overcast. The atmosphere was similar to that in a place where a decision has been taken, slightly dull when argument has died.

The hedges did need cutting back again, noted Miriam. The bottom of the lane beyond which stood her car in its primitive lay-by was almost barred by the thorn and briar. So that explained the scratches on Simon's arms. She could see the shepherd on the hillside through a dip in the hedge and the gamekeeper stood before her. Miriam wondered now why she was not and never had been afraid of him. She felt she should be as he loomed in front of her, cutting her off from her way to the road.

Despite his smallness of stature he seemed to dominate the lane.

'Good morning,' she said. She felt he was about to ask her where she thought she was going and that would have been frightening – very frightening indeed, although she did not know quite why – so she spoke again, rapidly. 'They're going out tonight,' she said. 'I've persuaded them to go out and I shall mind the baby.' She said, 'I'll be alone with the baby.'

And then she said, 'Of course, you will all be coming to see me.' And she wondered who she had meant by 'all', and yet on that other clouded level where she and he had communicated she knew, and knew she could have done no differently. If she had not invited them they would have come anyway and that would have been the most frightening of all.

'I'll cut back the thorns,' he said, and she saw he had in his hand a knife with a long, curved blade that gleamed with the sheen of water.

Miriam sighed. 'There is too much here that I do not understand,' she said, knowing that there was no sympathy in him and expecting none.

'I'll see you tonight,' he said like any ordinary man, but Miriam was not deceived. She thought it wiser not to tell the others that she had invited the local inhabitants for the evening. It might prevent them from going and nothing would be resolved. The die was cast and she was not the one to shirk responsibility. The Tylwyth Teg would be dropping in for a drink.

*

'Now you mustn't forget your coats,' said Miriam as evening approached. She said this not so much out of concern for the chills they might take from the insidious air as to remind them that they were going out: that there was no question about it, no room for discussion and no time for argument. The excursion was inevitable and they might as well be warm. So far she could discern no signs of rebellion but she was taking no chances. 'A scarf might be a good idea too,' she added considerately, 'to cover your ears.'

'You do fuss, Miriam,' said Clare amiably enough.

'And you ought to go quite soon,' continued Miriam. 'You don't want to have to wait for a table. You know how crowded these places get.' Despite her slight apprehension as to the evening which lay before her, she was glad she was not to be one of the party which must endure the thronging restaurant. But she had spoken unguardedly.

'I think I'd rather go to the pub,' said Clare.

'They don't do dinner at the pub,' said Miriam. 'You know that perfectly well, and the landlord's hands are dirty.' The habitués of the pub would be here in the red house and the pub would be echoingly empty. In such a case the few lonely visitors would soon grow bored and sullen and insist on buying a bottle to take home. Miriam did not want them home too early, for she knew on that other level, where reason bowed to a different dimension, that this could prove disastrous. She knew that the motive for sending them out had not arisen in herself but had been surreptitiously imposed on her, and far from being resentful she meant to make the most of what she perceived as an advantage. There was something going on and she would get to the bottom of it. Somebody had to.

'I don't think I'll come,' said Eloise, and Miriam realized that the baby had stopped howling. To her relief Clare took on the air of one about to put her foot down.

'You must,' she said with simple emphasis, for she was now eager for her night out and not enthusiastic at the prospect of spending it alone with young Simon. Three were almost invariably better company than two, especially for the one who found the others less than stimulating. Even if they both bored you nearly senseless they had each other to turn to, thus relieving you of the necessity of making superhuman efforts.

Miriam, just to be on the safe side, went into the parlour and pinched the baby. It gave her a look of cold hatred but it started to howl again. 'Good baby,' she said insincerely.

There is a nightmare, fairly common to those who have the care of an infant: that if they close their eyes for a second they will hear it walking about. It makes the blood run cold.

The baby had stopped crying the moment the others had left the house and Miriam had sunk into the parlour armchair. There was a silence and then the baby sat up and said, 'Have they gone?' and Miriam said, 'Yes,' and the baby said, 'So let's have a drink then,' and it climbed out of its cradle and waddled to the corner cupboard where the vodka was kept. Its silver hair hung down its back and its nappy hung to its knees. Miriam was not really surprised. She would be later when she thought about it, but the human mind has a tendency to accept the extraordinary at the time it is happening. It needs a while to explain to itself that this is impossible. The baby climbed back in its cradle with its bottle and proceeded to drink. It seemed not to be in the mood to converse, which was fortunate as Miriam found herself at a loss for words. She too felt the need for a drink but the baby was emptying the bottle.

When the Tylwyth Teg arrived – for now that Miriam had agreed to admit to herself that such they were, it seemed vain to deny it – the baby was slightly drunk but not incapable.

'So?' demanded Miriam, taking the initiative. The largest of them turned to her – the shepherd – or was he the doctor or the policeman or was he perhaps the High King? He said in his strange, precise English that something had gone a little wrong. Miriam appealed to the gamekeeper – the little one or the nurse or the other policeman or whatever he was. Of all of them he seemed the most accessible, as though he had a dash of human blood.

'She should not have brought it back to the house,' he said. 'She should have done as they all should do and left it by the waterfall. She would have wakened and thought she had dreamed it – as you will do.'

'I'm sure that's true,' agreed Miriam, 'but in the meantime it all seems rather too real.' Trust Eloise to give birth to a changeling and then refuse to abide by the conventions. 'If Eloise comes back and finds no baby, I could not answer for the consequences. She will undoubtedly alert the police, the Social Services . . .'

'We've come to change the baby,' said the two identical ones in concert, the social workers. They appeared to consider this a joke to be shared with a human and looked a little offended when Miriam failed to laugh. They themselves were laughing a lot.

'I see,' said Miriam. 'Nobody – that is nobody human – knows.' The laughter stopped. They all looked grave and shook their heads slowly as though in commiseration. Miriam hoped they were not insulted by her references to their non-humanity. They didn't seem to be. Hardly surprising, really, taking all in all, mused Miriam, her thoughts beginning to drift. 'It's happened before, hasn't it?' she said, recalling herself to reality, by which and by now she meant only what she supposed to be the present. 'Other women in this house have tried to keep the baby. What happened to them?' No one answered her but there rose from them a wail, a high keening – ooohhh – they mourned.

'All right,' said Miriam. 'All right.' The baby was staring at her with an expression of horrid interest as though gauging her reaction, the depth and degree and smell and texture of her fear. She cast it a look of contempt to let it know it had never deceived her and it didn't frighten her now. Although it did a little – oh, it really did.

'So what is to be done?' she asked carefully, now aware that they were not used on a regular basis to communicate in language – or none of which she was cognizant – and found it unnatural. For reassurance she spoke silently to herself – Miriam, she said, your choice of words leaves something to be desired. *Unnatural*. Define the word. In her own mind she must keep clear the boundaries between what was natural and what was not or find herself – or lose herself – in another dimension.

'She must give the baby back,' they said. Miriam was almost moved to protest here that it was not a baby but something quite different. It had a leer in its lake-green eyes and its silver hair needed combing.

'I couldn't agree with you more,' she said vigorously. 'I wish you could just take it away with you now.' Was it her imagination or did the baby look slightly annoyed? Certainly the men when they spoke spoke coldly. She must be wary, for she did not know what rules they observed. It would seem that they too, like humankind, were afflicted by pride and she must be more respectful of their unknown sensibilities.

They said no, they couldn't just take it – and were clearly not prepared to argue. Nor were they prepared to explain, although Miriam suspected that this was probably because they were unable. In such a culture clash neither party can be quite aware of what the other finds inexplicable. The problem arises even amongst human beings of different persuasions. A custom, the purpose of which is evident to one, can be baffling to another. People all over the world kept suggesting hopefully that they should sit down round a table and talk, but since no one knew what anyone else was talking about it was a sad waste of time. Even gestures, what some referred to as body language, could be misconstrued. For instance, it was inadvisable in an Arab country to beckon with the forefinger since to an Arab this meant something deeply offensive. Miriam's mind was wandering again.

At the sound of hoofbeats in the lane the baby rose to its feet, swaying as the cradle rocked. Miriam watched dispassionately, not inclined to leap to break its fall. It looked eager but the men shook their heads again and sighed – aaahhh. The baby sat down with a thud amidst the white lawn and lace and the cradle shook violently.

Miriam wished she could stop her thoughts straying. A woman of intelligence should be able to concentrate a little even in the most untoward of circumstances. The baby wanted to go into the night and leap on the back of the *ceffyl dŵr* and gallop away and away: its eyes were set on something distant and it slapped the flanks of its cradle and rocked back and forth. Miriam was almost sure she was right about this while conceding that she could be wrong. The baby might be thinking something quite different. She was going to make no more assumptions but be entirely passive in thought and deed. She merely looked inquiringly at the large man and awaited instructions. Any attempt at assertiveness would be self-defeating.

The instructions were simple: they, that is the women, had to take the baby to the top of the waterfall and throw it down. This seemingly drastic measure was, it appeared, all that would suffice. She turned to the gamekeeper who was no longer smiling. He bared his teeth briefly without enthusiasm. They were growing impatient.

'I'll do it now,' offered Miriam recklessly, but they shook their heads.

'All the women,' said the gamekeeper, 'or they might remember. Sometimes they do and that is . . .' he sought for a word, '. . . unfortunate.' Miriam could see what he meant. Collusion was called for here, if forgetfulness were to follow. They understood more of human nature than she had given them credit for. Not one of the women was to be permitted to stand aloof from the act for even if, as seemed unlikely, she fully understood the necessity for it she might, in the course of time, see fit to criticize and that would be in no one's interests.

'Then I have only one question,' said Miriam, enunciating clearly. 'How am I to put it to Eloise?'

'Give her a drink,' said the twins, laughing again. The large man imperceptibly reverted to his persona as a man of medicine.

'Give her this,' he advised, and he passed across the vodka bottle which the baby had emptied. It was full again. 'You must all drink it,' he said. Miriam thought that nothing would persuade her to imbibe fairy vodka but she did not say so.

'I'll take them for a picnic,' she said, 'but you'd better leave before they come back. And make the baby go to sleep.' It was still rocking and she was beginning to feel a little sorry for it. 'And what about Simon?' she asked. 'What will Simon say?'

'He won't even notice,' said the twins. One of them cuffed the baby on the side of the head and it lay down. They left, laughing. It was hours before the cat came back.

Clare returned in an ugly mood. She had had too much and not enough to drink and her dinner had given her indigestion. All evening she had thought of Claud dining in some *soigné* little place surrounded by famous people, while she dined virtually alone, exiled among people no one had ever heard of. She didn't consider Eloise and Simon to be company. They were just there. She had, against all likelihood, entertained a tiny hope that she might meet a man. A fairy prince was too much to expect, but surely she might have been permitted an actor, a writer, someone scouring the countryside in search of a suitable location for something. Even a businessman provided he was well past middle-management. No one resembling any of these had been present. Only couples of the sort who roamed the theme parks, their only purpose to consume. Clare felt cheated.

'Do you ever get the feeling there are no real people left?' she demanded. Miriam jumped. But Clare went on. 'They all look like characters in the most ghastly soap opera and they read newspapers and magazines about people in soap operas. The very far gone send flowers when the characters die, while the real people – whoever they are – are acting in panto or drying out somewhere. Did you know there are cafés done up like film sets and people pretend to be film stars and say things to you? They must get awfully fed up with it, saying the same old lines.'

Miriam relaxed. If anyone apart from herself suspected they had been mingling with fairies then matters would become inextricably confused. 'It's probably the latest manifestation of the human urge to self-destruction. As the man said, "Humankind cannot bear too much reality." Virtual Reality isn't so demanding. You can switch off and not have to shoot yourself to get out.'

'You couldn't have a conversation with any of them,' grumbled Clare, loosening her scarf. 'You wouldn't know where they were in the script. *They'd* think *you* were crazy.' The injustice of this rankled painfully. 'They're living in another world,' she said.

'The problem of objective reality,' said Miriam tactfully, 'is one that has troubled the greatest philosophical

183

minds throughout the ages.' Clare was mollified and went quite peacefully to bed.

Miriam turned to Simon, for Eloise had gone to the baby. While she was preoccupied with the question of how to suggest to a mother that her only sensible course was to drop her baby down a waterfall, she yet had to do what she could to preserve some illusion of normality. 'Did you have a nice time?' she asked. Simon looked at her uncomprehendingly, as though her question were meaningless. She couldn't blame him.

'Yes, thank you,' he said, due to his having been so well brought up. Untypically Miriam wished briefly that he had been raised in a rather more open fashion. It was difficult to speak of profoundly unusual matters to a well-mannered person. She persevered, determined not to reveal the full extent of the oddness of their circumstances, yet curious to know whether Simon had noticed anything.

'Was it not a relief to get away from the house for a while?' she inquired.

'It was very kind of you,' said Simon. Miriam was mortified: he thought she was soliciting his gratitude. There was nothing she could add without saying too much. 'Did you know your child was a changeling?' was not a good conversational gambit, and if she questioned him further about his evening he would conclude that she was avid for more appreciation. She felt protective towards him and told him to go to bed. Women, while not exactly designed for dealing with the chaotic, yet were more suited to the task than men, who were poorly equipped to cope with bewilderment and sulked or grew belligerent when faced with the inexplicable. It was probably because they did not care for the sensation of powerlessness, thought Miriam charitably.

The baby was quiet now. 'Thank you,' said Simon again, pausing as he went upstairs. Really, a dear boy, thought Miriam. It was too bad of Eloise to have dragged him into this confusion. She felt wakeful and alert and disinclined to sleep. The night was extraordinarily quiet. She went and put her ear to the parlour door, listening to hear how Eloise and the baby were comporting themselves on their last night together. There was no sound. Half against her will she opened the door a crack and peered round. Eloise sat in a shaft of moonlight, cross-legged on the lace strewn sofa, gazing down at the cradle. As Miriam watched she reached down and rocked it gently, slowly, and as it turned towards her Miriam saw the baby's face illumined by the moon, its eyes shining. It closed one in a leisurely wink and Miriam backed silently away.

She sat up all night, staring at the kitchen window, scarcely expecting the dawn ever to break. When it did she was quite surprised. She washed her face hurriedly at the kitchen sink and opened the door on the morning: a dear little morning – she thought, suspicious of its innocent aspect. She thought of old, evil things dressed up in lightly coloured gauzes that should only be permitted to the young, the faultless, so that there should be no deception. Through the insubstantial drifting clouds, palely stained with pink; the palely purple shadows, transparent as air, she could still discern the lineaments of wickedness. At another time she might have attributed this jaundiced view to the state of her liver, but not now. Admittedly she had been drinking more than was usual to her, but alcoholic depression was not the cause of her unease. An awareness had been forced upon her of a world careless of mankind, more terrible than malice in its indifference. No, she mused, it was not after all wickedness that hung in the sweet air, infused the pasture and the dappling woods and informed the mute hedgerows. It was absence. The absence of cognizance, of love, of all that mankind might call God.

She was aroused from her melancholy reverie by a cross voice. 'I said – shall I make the tea?' demanded Clare, obviously for the second, or perhaps the third, time. 'You were miles away. I thought you'd died on your feet, like a horse.'

'I think they only sleep standing up,' said Miriam, glad of the distraction. 'They fall over when they die, like the rest of us.'

'Well, I didn't get up this early to talk about dead horses,' said Clare. 'We have to decide what to do. I want to go home. I find the country peculiar. You've got to talk to Eloise.' By this, of course, she meant that Miriam should persuade Eloise to do as her mother bade.

'Talking's no use,' said Miriam.

'So what do you suggest?' asked Clare, as though the whole matter were Miriam's responsibility. Which indeed it was, thought Miriam. Only Clare didn't know that. She took too much for granted.

'We're going on a picnic today,' she announced, 'and don't start asking why because I know what I'm doing. Just do as I say.'

'You can be awfully bossy, you know,' remarked Clare argumentatively. Miriam battled with mounting exasperation.

'Do you want an end to all this or not?' she inquired.

'Yes,' agreed Clare meekly. She didn't want to madden Miriam. She was puzzled by this talk of picnics, but since in the past she had always found her friend reliable, she would just have to trust her. There was nothing else that she could think of.

'We'll go to that place by the waterfall you said would be so perfect for a picnic,' said Miriam.

'But there's a dead – sheep – there,' objected Clare before she could stop herself.

'No, there isn't,' said Miriam. 'The shepherd told the gamekeeper and the gamekeeper took it away. Every bit.' Clare wanted to ask how she knew but deemed it wiser to keep her mouth shut.

Miriam was beginning to think that everything was progressing smoothly when Simon came downstairs and said he wasn't going to work today. He thought he must have eaten something the night before. He and Clare embarked on the usual fruitless discussion, common in cases of food poisoning, as to whether they had had the same items at dinner or whether the cause might lie in something he had ingested at lunch. Miriam interrupted to insist that he return to bed at once and stay there. All day. It would seriously interfere with her plans should he express a desire to accompany the women on their picnic. She spoke with emphasis, in the tone of a woman whose will must not be denied, and Simon obeyed.

'You *are* bossy,' said Clare, rather admiringly this time.

'Someone has to be,' said Miriam. She was already finding the role of commanding officer irksome but there was nothing to be done about it.

Eloise came into the kitchen carrying her baby. Its silver head lolled on her shoulder and Miriam could only see its back. It seemed the back of a tiny, a new-born, child and Miriam felt suddenly sick. Her sight dimmed and she grew pale.

'Are you all right?' cried Clare, alarmed, and even Eloise, preoccupied as she was, stepped closer to look at Miriam. As they leaned towards her the baby lifted its head and turned, and again, looking straight at her, closed one green eye.

'Yes, I'm all right,' said Miriam.

Eloise and Clare took it in turns to carry the baby up the lane to the appointed place. If they found it strange that

Miriam did not offer to share the burden they said nothing. She was carrying the picnic basket laden with ham sandwiches and cold sausages, a jar of artichoke hearts from Fortnum's and a cheese sandwich for herself, although she had no appetite, and the bottle of fairy vodka. It was hot for early autumn and a haze shimmered before them. As they climbed higher the haze cleared and the light grew dazzlingly bright.

'I didn't bring my sunglasses,' grumbled Clare, 'and I can hardly see a thing.'

'Just as well,' said Miriam. 'Just as well.'

'What?' said Clare.

'Nothing,' said Miriam.

When they reached the dell the sun was shining – it seemed to Miriam obsessively – into its centre. 'Sit in the shade,' she directed peremptorily. Eloise put the baby down under an old, twisted blackthorn and sat beside it.

Miriam was about to suggest a drink when Clare demanded one. As she lifted the bottle from the basket Miriam wondered whether she should say something a little disparaging in order to contribute a semblance of normality to the scene, something not too condemnatory about the earliness of the hour and incipient alcoholism. Would they expect it of her? She could not decide whether it was too late for pretence or whether she should continue to act as though nothing were amiss. She did not know in which dimension the other two were breathing on this particular day when all her own perceptions and responses were as out of sequence as a carelessly dropped deck of cards. As she poured the vodka into two plastic cups Clare asked petulantly whether she were not having one herself. Miriam hesitated. A draught of fairy liquor might be just what she needed; might rid her of her inhibitions, might bring her to a condition where the untoward seemed natural: for, while convinced of the course that must be taken, she yet could not rid herself of the awareness that it was not the act of a normal woman to throw a baby down a waterfall.

'No,' she said, thinking that she must keep a clear head, not abrogate responsibility, no matter what the cost to her self-esteem, her sanity. 'I'll just have a tonic.' But as she was engaged in unpacking the basket of sandwiches, twisting the top of the jar of artichokes, Clare poured a hasty measure of vodka into the third plastic cup. She had the remnants of a hangover which made her feel spiteful and disinclined to let her friend perch in solitary purity on the moral high ground. Miriam drank it.

The colours of the day altered, deepening and brightening. The light leapt and shifted, shattering into faceted fragments, and her spirits rose. There were no shadows now and Miriam began to feel wise and powerful. Everything seemed right. Clare, noting the alteration in her friend's demeanour, cast a wink at Eloise, seeking complicity in her trivial act of insurrection. The baby, intercepting the wink, closed one green and glittering eye and grinned.

'It smiled at me,' said Clare, 'but I suppose it's only wind.'

'I'm going to look at the waterfall,' said Miriam. She didn't invite the others to accompany her since that would give them the opportunity to decline. Left to themselves they would follow. They looked dazed and heavy-eyed but they got to their feet. Miriam found herself feeling far from steady but her resolution held firm.

When they stood at the top of the waterfall the light grew ever wilder, now revealing hidden hollows in the ancient, unvisited wood; now blinding the mortals, confounding their expectations with its unaccustomed waywardness.

'Look,' said Clare, 'there's a horse.'

'It's a rock,' said Miriam, but she too could see it below them in the dark pool, its silver white mane streaming out in the falling water, white foam along its gleaming flanks, glass green eyes shining in the broken light and its head turning up towards them. It reared, once – twice – flailing unshod, scarlet hooves, and the baby leapt in Eloise's arms.

She clutched at it but it was no longer soft, no longer small. She was fighting to hold on to something that did not love her, something that sprang from her arms with a great howl of triumph and leapt down, down to the water that leapt up to meet it.

*

'I must have dropped off,' said Miriam. 'What's the time?' She lay in the glade which was paling as evening drew on, the surrounding ferns curling their fronds into tiny fists. She sat up and looked round. The evidence of their picnic lay round her: greasy paper, plastic cup, empty bottle. 'How disgusting,' she said, feeling like a defiler, a tourist. They must have eaten everything although she had no recollection of having done so. They must have drunk all the vodka. That would account for her forgetfulness.

'What are you doing?' asked Clare, sitting up in her turn.

'I'm tidying up,' said Miriam, putting the horrid detritus into the basket, determined to remove all traces of their presence. She felt, without knowing why, that it was part of a bargain.

'Where's Eloise?' Clare now asked, making, Miriam noted, no move to help restore order.

They found her sitting at the top of the waterfall. 'There's a lamb caught in the rushes,' she said, her eyes fixed on something downstream.

'There aren't any lambs at this time of year,' her mother informed her.

'I can see it,' insisted Eloise. 'We must go and get it.'

'It's only foam,' said Miriam, 'only foam caught in the rushes,' and as she spoke a sudden eddy caught it so that it dispersed and drifted away. Eloise sighed and the evening breeze softly lifted her hair.

'We must hurry,' said Miriam. 'We've left Simon alone

too long.' She felt suddenly uneasy, aware of urgency, a need for haste. As they reached the top of the lane Eloise pointed downwards.

'Look,' she said. 'There are my men.' The four were visible in the distance clustered at the gate of Ty Coch. There was a gleam about them in the gathering dusk. The whiteness of their shirts, said Miriam's common sense. The lustre of metal in the last shaft of sunlight said something else.

'Hurry,' she cried, beginning to run down the pitted lane. She had never cared for the sound of Eloise's men. Eloise hung back.

'We've forgotten something,' she said. 'I know we've forgotten something.' Miriam raced on, careless of the risk of stumbling, unafraid of the four. She somehow knew it had never been women who were endangered in the red house. She lost sight of it at the turn in the lane and when she arrived the men had gone.

'Simon,' she called. 'Simon.'

'What the hell's the hurry?' demanded Clare, coming up behind her, panting. Like all people, like all sheep, she had run when she saw Miriam running, afraid of she knew not what unsuspected threat. 'And what the hell are you doing?' she asked through her breathlessness as she perceived Simon trying to conceal himself behind the kitchen door.

Simon blushed. 'I was asleep,' he said, 'and I had nothing on and there was a knock at the door, so I grabbed the first thing that came to hand.' He was wearing one of Eloise's nightdresses, befrilled and laced and falling in full folds to his ankles.

'It doesn't suit you,' said Clare, falling into a chair. Simon's blush intensified.

It was hard to gauge his state of mind from his demeanour: there was a lump rising on his left temple and he looked dazed.

'What's that bump on your head?' asked Miriam. Simon began hesitatingly to explain. He had been asleep and had heard someone moving about downstairs. He had had no clothes on and had seized the nearest garment, which had chanced to be one of Eloise's nightdresses. As he ran downstairs he had tripped on its hem and fallen and banged his head. The front door had been open and there were men standing there. One was already in the hallway, menacing and moving towards him, and he had been mortally afraid.

'They must have been burglars,' Simon said, 'from the town, looking for antiques.' He paused. Already the memory was fading, but as he had risen to his feet and the men saw him in his nightgowned entirety, they had stopped and exchanged wild glances, not of mirth but of bewilderment, of fearful incomprehension.

'Then I passed out,' he continued, 'and when I came to they'd gone.'

'Then it's back to bed for you,' announced Miriam. 'Do you want any help?' Simon, who had been about to protest, thought it simpler to comply. Besides, he was eager to discard the nightdress – it was interfering with his sense of identity.

'Simon's been behaving very oddly,' said Clare. 'He's got very accident prone and they're both far too young to live all alone in this God-forsaken dump. I'm not going away without them. There's a peculiar atmosphere here. You get the feeling anything could happen. And what if Eloise got pregnant?'

'Yes, what?' echoed Miriam, who had an exasperating sensation that she'd missed something. Small shards of memory came and went in her mind, almost within her conscious grasp and gone again before she could clothe them in words. It was as though she had been drunk or drugged and time had circled round her and gone on. Since she was unaware of having taken anything which might bring her to this state she felt anxious and in need of release, of the stimulus of city life: living in the country where anything could happen and nothing ever did undoubtedly addled the brain. She went to put the kettle on.

Later in the evening Eloise ran away. Clare went into the kitchen to ascertain who was going to make supper and found her standing at the doorway to the garden with her arms held out to the thickening darkness. 'Is there anything special you'd like for supper?' Clare had asked elliptically and Eloise had leaped like a startled member of some species of deer and run into the descending night. Clare had run after her. She had hesitated at the edge of the woods and called softly – but a whisper was an inadequate vehicle for her feelings, and if she should express them at the pitch they required Miriam would say she was hysterical. Making her way through the trees, first moving to the left, she hissed, 'Eloise, Eloise,' but the only sound she heard when she stopped, and the rustle caused by her movements stopped, was the sound of other rustles caused by the movements of something else. She preferred not to hear these alien rustles and turned back in the direction of the house, but then she tripped against a fallen bough and turned again and was lost.

'Who's there?' she asked in a normal voice which did not sound normal when she heard it. She wondered what her words meant, 'Who's there, there's who . . .?' They seemed meaningless. A mere panic attack, Clare assured herself. She had never before suffered such a thing but had frequently been subjected to descriptions of the consternation they could cause. She knew that she should now put her head in a brown paper bag, but she hadn't got one. Few people ever had, walking in the woods at night, she told herself sensibly, wondering what happened next. The trees seemed to be growing more closely together and the ground was uneven and loosely woven with trailing strands that caught at her feet. Again she wondered how it would end, this emptiness composed of nothing but terror. A terror which existed in nothing but herself – which relied on nothing but her. Then she found the trees growing less intimately and the ground rising: looking up she could see stars shining through the branches, and led by that instinct that compels you from the heart of the forest towards any space or light, she went forwards and upwards.

By the time she reached the clearing the moon was risen. Clare was not surprised by the presence of the gamekeeper. Had he been anyone else she might – who knows – have given way to fear, but whereas it would have been odd to discover, say, a baker or a plumber on a moonlit mountainside, it was perfectly in order to meet the gamekeeper. Especially if you saw him first. If she had turned to find him behind her, she *might* have died.

'I'm looking for my daughter,' she said, but the wind was rising and singing with the water and her words were inaudible. She leaned towards him and said more loudly, 'I'm looking for my daughter.' He seemed un-certain how to respond and took a step back. Clare was the taller and as terrible as any mother seeking her child. The wind died down for a moment and he said he knew nothing of daughters. Clare stepped even closer so that for a moment they shared a breath. She said in a voice that neither the wind nor the water could overcome that there was a rapist at large and her daughter was alone and lost in this filthy wilderness – with its bogs and precipices to add to the disadvantages. She said that wild horses would not get her off this mountainside without her daughter.

The gamekeeper seemed inordinately affected by the

mention of wild horses: he looked inquiringly into Clare's eyes as though wondering how much she knew. It was he who had been primarily responsible for the recent events at Ty Coch; he always had been, all through the centuries, and it had never been pleasant when he got things wrong. Ever since the time all those years and years before when the men of the Tylwyth Teg had been out hunting and a peripatetic holy man had come across the Queens dancing with their women and banished them, exorcized them with one stroke before he passed on to wreak more havoc throughout the old land.

Ever since they had had to rely on the daughters of humankind to perpetuate their own kind and it had become increasingly difficult. Once those humans who lived in the place where the Queens and their women had danced had been feared and spurned by their fellows; some who had been rejected by the human race were left to wander, wild-eyed, through the woods and fields, homeless. As time went by and the humans grew more what they were eventually to describe as 'civilized', they sometimes burned the women as witches possessed by the devil, for the women were always strange. Later on, as they grew more enlightened and didn't really believe in witches any more, they hanged them for infanticide when the mothers were incautious and revealed that they had borne a child who later was nowhere to be seen. Sometimes they hanged them for murder, for the Tylwyth Teg would not permit the presence of human males where the Queens had lived, and there were numerous cases of mysterious disappearances and curious deaths among the husbands and the wives were always blamed for these mishaps.

And now it was almost impossible to make new Tylwyth Teg. Not that it was difficult to find willing human women. No. It was easier now than it had been for several centuries and they needed little persuasion, often not needing the assistance of applied magic. The difficulty lay in securing secrecy, since the hated 'civilization' had become something called bureaucracy and nobody's life or death was his own. If a passer-by should notice a woman behaving oddly he would mention it to someone in the village, who would mention it to some minor official, who would start thinking in terms of forms and be up at Ty Coch before you could turn round. In the old days the local people had dealt with affairs in their own straightforward way. The gamekeeper found it incomprehensible – the conflict in the human race between its passion for interference and its basic indifference to its members. Not that he cared. He didn't think in human terms. Humans were useful for breeding when you could catch one, and every now and then when it seemed safe he ate one, but otherwise he avoided them on the whole . . .

'Where's my daughter?' said Clare, who had remained in the sort of Greenwich Mean Time she was familiar with as the gamekeeper brooded. She said in a very stern tone, 'Where in the name of God is my daughter?' The gamekeeper jumped at the Name he feared and hated above all else. It was in that Name that all the trouble had started. 'The rapist is around here somewhere,' said Clare. 'I know it in my bones.'

The gamekeeper clutched the place where his heart would have been if he'd had one. He had picked up the gesture from a woman of the house some hundreds of years ago, finding it faintly intriguing. 'Down there,' he said before he could consider its consequences.

Clare began to slide down the bank to where Eloise was quietly polishing off what was left of the rapist.

'What do you think you're doing, in the name of . . .?' she began, before the gamekeeper hastily interrupted in case she should use *that* Name again.

'*Ach y fi*,' he said, bending down to remove the knuckle bone from Eloise's mouth before her mother should see it. He dropped it on the mossy bank and wondered what to do next.

'What are you doing?' demanded Clare again, standing with her hands on her hips and her feet apart in the attitude of every furious mother since time began and people came to measure it.

'Waiting for the baby,' said Eloise. 'Look, there's the horse.' *She* spoke as any mother might speak, watching her child reappear on its skateboard round the laurel in the park. Clare swung round, caught a brief glimpse of a white horse which instantly transmuted itself into the fallen, whitened branch of a rowan, and swung back.

'What baby?' she inquired.

The gamekeeper considered that the time for action had come. He was aware that he himself was now being watched and it was not a comforting knowledge. His brethren relied on their leaders, their Kings, to protect them from inconvenience and could be very cold if they considered they had been let down. He had made mistakes: the chief among them the failure to realize that Eloise had something of the Tylwyth Teg in her – more than he had suspected was possible in a so-called human, and was both susceptible and immune to his magic.

Regretfully he must now resort to coarser methods and avail himself of Eloise's human vulnerability. The Tylwyth Teg had great faith, formed over the centuries from observation, in the amnesiac effects of a blow to the human head. So he surreptitiously sprinkled fairy dust on Clare's cropped hair so that some fell into her eyes and some in her ears, and he clouted Eloise behind the ear with a nice round stone.

There was no problem getting them home. Clare and Eloise were carried back by a wild, white horse.

Meanwhile Miriam was enduring a misunderstanding with the shepherd. Having discovered, at what she thought must be supper time, that Clare and Eloise were missing, she had gone to look for them, leaving Simon to sleep off his concussion. Poor Simon. It was later than she thought and nearly dark when she reached the turn in the lane and bumped into the shepherd. He was not in a good humour, for the plan had failed. Eloise had remembered. At this very moment she was playing with the baby in the woods by the stream, unconscious of the cold or the dark, eating fairy food. Once upon a time it would not have mattered. They would have left her alone, hidden the baby from her and let her roam until she died – of exposure or the claws and teeth of the wild beasts or starvation or grief – it was all the same to them. The man they would have killed and disposed of in some way or another, depending on the state of the fairy larders, and the women they would have left to go mad. But that was in the old days. They had learned painfully that these casual expedients no longer applied. There were eyes everywhere.

Engaged in that wearisome and embarrassing dance of a couple facing each other in a narrow space, each wishing to move onwards, Miriam wondered why he appeared so disapproving. She stepped unwillingly on to the grass that bordered the lane to let him pass and was stung by a nettle. 'Ouch,' she said. He didn't move or speak so it became essential for Miriam to say more. She chose the harmless words, 'I'm just looking for my friends,' and was taken aback when he failed to answer but glared down at her. He was larger than she remembered and his dog was nastier, slinking and growling, its lips lifted in a threatening sneer. Miriam, unaware that she had so recently entertained him in the red house, was baffled by his behaviour. She had gone to such pains to be civil to the indigenous population. The shepherd, who had never had much personal acquaintance with human beings, was assuming that since one remembered, then so must they all. The Tylwyth Teg thought and moved alike, barely grasping the concept of the individual. The High King imagined himself and his subjects insulted. He was not the most intelligent of elementals. Miriam broke free from the goose-grass that seized her skirt and the mist that clouded her mind and went on.

The shepherd stood brooding. The last time they had blundered had been around the turn of the century. Until then few people had ventured near their territory, since from before time was it had been theirs, a place where no one not of the Order dared go, a place of sacrifice. Sometimes unwary peasants, driven by poverty to wander, had flung up, overnight, a Ty Nos. If they could get the chimney up before daybreak they were legally entitled (by the laws of men) to live there. Few had stayed long. Then had come young people, two of them, and they had brought outsiders to build anew the last house. It took some time because the outsiders kept running away and being replaced by others. The Kings, unaccustomed to intrusion and the unreliability of builders, had watched for a while helpless and amazed. The young people had come from far away, from what was called 'city', to find what was called 'the simple life'. The villagers, xenophobes to a man, had been overcome by mistrust, at the same time as resentment that outsiders had been employed in their part of the country, and would go nowhere near them. The young man had been a sculptor in wood and delved in the garden while his wife span. They had eaten only grasses and things that grew in the fields, and such crops as they could grow themselves and they looked pale; and after a while two more women came to join them. For a while the Tylwyth Teg had been intrigued by their antics, for they were the followers of one Madame Blavatsky and called themselves theosophists and sought to perform occult practices and commune with nature. They held seances and afforded the fairies a good deal of mirth by contriving to extrude, from parts of their persons, lengths of muslin which they called ectoplasm, and using strange voices which they represented as their spirit guides – usually a Red Indian called Sitting Bull or something. The girl had worn homespun and amber beads and gone round barefoot, talking to the flowers. They believed in reincarnation, communed with the Earth Mother, wore sandals and were fond of nuts.

And after another while had passed and the humans went nowhere and no one came to see them, it had occurred to the Kings that they could use the young woman. It would be easier than altering their appearance and going to the town for the yearly fair and coaxing away a servant girl for hire. But it was then they should have learned their lesson, for when the girl refused to return the child and, perforce, drowned in the stream, the humans in the house had raised a hue and cry and caused the fairies great perplexity as more and more humans trampled the land searching for her and the child. They were forced to the boundaries, from where they could only watch.

It was all right in the end, since when the commotion died down and the searchers left, leaving only the villagers, no one went near Ty Coch. Only the gossip and whispered rumours remained and stayed on ... Rumours of events that broke nearly every commandment and some that God hadn't even bothered to specify. But the Kings were indifferent to this aspect, *never* thinking of God if they could help it. The men of the locality especially feared the red house.

When Miriam had gone on the shepherd turned towards it.

Simon woke at the sound of something moving in the garden beneath his window. He got out of bed and pulled on his pants and shirt. The house was eerily quiet without the sound of women's voices, and the light of the moon was fitful. The trees seemed no more substantial than their shadows and Simon thought deeply before making any further movement. Great responsibility lay on the first person to disturb an absolute stillness. Someone had to, Simon reminded himself and he put his head out of the window and asked who was there. He became conscious that the silence held a faintly offended, quality, evocative of Eloise's brief sulks.

'Eloise?' he called, and when there was no answer he went downstairs and opened the kitchen door to discover the shepherd leaning against the jamb, unsmiling. Simon, who had not known what to expect, was relieved to see a familiar face. The thought that it was rather too familiar, occurring unexpectedly on different people, went through his mind yet again, but was swiftly dismissed in favour of the rational theory of the consequences of intermarriage. He automatically adopted an expression of enlightened forbearance, very trying to the recipient, whatever his nature and condition.

The conversation that ensued was confusing to both parties, one being, as the old Welsh saying had it, in the *cae tatws* – which is the potato field – and the other in the field of turnips. Simon was as yet too young and inexperienced to have realized how frequently two people who imagine they are addressing the same matter are approaching it from such disparate angles that they are out even of shouting distance – and the shepherd, incapable of ever quite grasping the ways of men, was too remote and uninformed. So, given over to the fairies' unquestioning assumption that mortal man was hostile, he abandoned pretence and carried on not smiling, tired of mimicking the mortals who were getting in his way.

Simon, unaware of the depth of misunderstanding, beamed. The shepherd, considering this insolent, took a threatening step forward. Simon stepped back with a welcoming gesture and asked if he'd care for a drink. The shepherd tried to think of a response and grew perceptibly taller.

'Mind your head,' said Simon caringly. 'Would you like tea or something stronger?' The shepherd grew icy with wrath. 'Brr,' said Simon, shutting the door. 'The nights are getting colder.' The shepherd wondered whether to strangle him or force upon him a dose of fairy death dust. Simon invited him to sit down.

'Where are your women?' asked the shepherd, his voice choked with a variety of fairy emotions.

'Don't let *them* hear you talking like that,' advised Simon, putting on the kettle and laughing a little. 'On the other hand,' he added, 'now I come to think about it, I wish I knew.' He stood still and reflected. 'What's the time?' The shepherd flexed his fingers. He wanted to say something clever and devastating about there not *being* any time and that what there was was time for Simon to DIE, but he doubted his ability to get it right or sufficiently alarming for someone who was as stupid as this young man appeared to be. He was convinced that Simon knew perfectly well that two of his women were tranced in the garden and the third was on her way back down the lane in a bad temper. The young man was mocking him with a pretence of indifference. He could feel his powers weakening.

Simon, who was beginning to enjoy this little chat, man to man with no women to interrupt, said rather regretfully that when they'd had their tea they'd better have a look round. See if the car was there, or if the girls had gone out for the evening without telling him. He remarked jovially, with the kindly intention of complimenting his slightly retarded visitor on his profession, that after all the Lord was their shepherd and they were probably negotiating their way home in the dark through green pastures – and when he turned he found himself alone. Puzzled, he opened the door and heard fading into the distance a howl of wrath, laced with lamentation.

Miriam arrived at the house, scratched and muddy and in a foul humour. A shapeless beast had swept past, forcing her into the ditch where all was slimy. The harvest moon was now shining brightly and she discerned Clare and Eloise immediately, the former lying with her head on the table and the latter stretched out comfortably on the grass. Simon was in the kitchen looking for sugar to put in his tea. It was not an altogether normal scene.

'What are you doing?' she demanded, hobbling into the kitchen.

'I can't find the sugar,' said Simon.

'Why are they sleeping in the garden?' asked Miriam.

'I don't know,' said Simon. 'I just woke up.'

'Then you'd better wake them up,' said Miriam. 'They've been drinking.'

The next day was dreary with a grey dampness and an unexpected razor-edged wind. The last straw came when the kitchen roof fell off. It was made of tarred felt, weighted down with large stones, and it all fell off, sliding with a certain sullen, subdued dignity into the garden.

'There,' said Eloise in wifely tones of bitter satisfaction. 'I knew it would do that if you didn't do something about it.' Simon maintained a sensible silence, looking up at the clouded sky.

'Well, that's about it,' said Clare. 'Time to go home, I think.'

Eloise had automatically begun to open her mouth, either to contradict or defy her mother – whatever negative response might be appropriate – but on reflection she changed her mind. She was, she admitted to herself, sick of the simple life. It had not been what she had expected. Here was a heaven-sent opportunity to get herself out of it without looking a dope. Even the most ardent pagan could not be expected to live in a house with no roof on the kitchen. So ran her thoughts. Miriam, observing her, saw the mutinous set of her mouth relax, and said a short but fervent prayer that Clare would not now ruin everything by insisting that her daughter do what she had already decided on doing.

'Tea?' invited Miriam. 'Shall we have a cup of tea before it rains?'

'Good idea,' said Clare hastily, as conscious as her friend of the need for speed and the extreme inadvisability of 'settling down to talk about this' – a course so beloved of the human race that it held almost sacred connotations, and was almost invariably disastrous. 'Let's get going. You make the tea and I'll start packing.' Clare was indeed taking this seriously, thought Miriam. She usually managed to get someone else to pack for her.

'You can sell the house with all its contents,' Clare said looking round as the dust settled. 'You just have to say "ripe for development and improvement with many original features" and "unspoiled country views".' 'Especially through the kitchen ceiling,' interrupted Miriam gloomily.

'There's nothing of any value here. It doesn't look as though you brought anything with you. Did you?' continued Clare.

'Only my sewing machine,' said Eloise. Clare extended her investigation into the parlour.

'It looks like a cemetery tip,' she said, eyeing with distaste the wilting greenery that festooned the little room. 'And what's this doing here?' she demanded, aiming a modest kick at the cradle standing on the floor. It rocked to and fro and for a second Miriam almost remembered something.

'Hush,' she said, closing her eyes, and then, 'No, it's no use. It's gone.'

'What?' asked Clare, staring at her.

'Nothing,' said Miriam.

'What's this nasty old thing doing here?' Clare called again. Eloise came into the parlour.

'It's for when I have a baby,' she explained. 'I got it ready for the baby.'

'When and if you have a baby,' said Clare, 'it will sleep in a nice clean cot . . .' She meant to say more but she too had been touched by the swift wing of passing memory and frowned in frustration as it disappeared into the dark. She shivered. 'The sooner we go the better.'

Miriam paused for a moment to examine her sense of urgency and realized that it was not the sort that hastens you towards the future – to an appointment or a con-summation – but an aspect of dread that bids you begone and leave behind unholy things. She spoke severely to herself about the disadvantages of thoughtless hurry and went to pack, ensuring that she picked up everything. She did not want to come back to the red house.

Eloise was listless and had raised no objection to their precipitate departure. It was as though she had already left in spirit and was prepared to follow in body without protest, without regret. Miriam found her attitude convenient but unnatural and became in consequence abnormally executive. 'Have you emptied all the drawers?' she demanded. 'Do you want to take any of the china? Have you left anything in the wardrobe? Where is the cat's basket? Where is the cat?' Clare was fretful.

'You are *bossy*, Miriam,' she said. 'Let's just *go*.'

'We can't go without the cat,' said Miriam crossly, 'and where's Simon? Shouldn't he put a tarpaulin over the kitchen?'

Clare said bother the kitchen but conceded that they couldn't go without Simon. They found him in the box-room, on his knees by Clare's bed. He turned to look at them as they stood in the doorway. 'M'sieu's had a kitten,' he said. 'Its eyes are open. He – I mean she,' he amended, 'must have had it days ago and just carried it in here.'

'M'sieu's a boy,' said Clare.

'No, he isn't,' said Simon, holding up the kitten as evidence. It had green, shining eyes.

On the way home Clare was visited by inspiration. The more she thought about it, the more she disliked the memory of the red house. 'They want to make a quick sale,' she told Miriam.

'I know what you're going to say,' said Miriam. 'Sell it to Fruitbat.'

'I suppose it's obvious,' said Clare. 'They're made for each other. There's more sheer, uninterrupted, boring, natural nature round there than I've seen on TV or anywhere. It wouldn't half serve her right.'

For the first time since leaving London Eloise sat beside Simon in the van. M'sieu and her kitten lay in a basket on a bed of white linen. M'sieu purred contentedly.

Eloise looked out at the unfamiliar countryside speeding by. Simon broke the silence. 'Kitten's happy,' he said.

'We've forgotten something,' said Eloise.

Afterword

Published in England in 1996, *Fairy Tale* is Alice Thomas Ellis's most recent novel. Although nineteen years and, by my count, nineteen other books stand between it and her first novel, *The Sin Eater*, such are the vagaries of publishers' timetables that I write these words almost immediately after having composed a brief afterword to that brilliant first. Does more than quirky scheduling make this pairing apropos?

One reason to think so is the novels' shared Welsh setting. In both stories a house in Wales draws city dwellers into the country, and what they (or at least the more perceptive of them) find there is anything but rural bliss. In *The Sin Eater* the intensity and the disconcerting lyricism of Ellis's descriptive passages give nature a shimmering menace; as filtered through the uneasy thoughts and perceptions of Rose and Ermyn, it is as vivid, bright, and colorful as a poisonous flower. And a menacing presence seems to attend it, a presence Ermyn becomes uncomfortably aware of, for example, when she enters the secluded field on which the book's climactic cricket match is to be played: "The blind blankness of the place made her feel that somewhere there must be an unseen watcher."

In *Fairy Tale* – a fairy tale for adults – that watcher is many watchers, and from the book's first sentence the reader sees them at their "inimical appraisal." Ty Coch, the enchanting little house of red brick, sits in its isolated Welsh valley under the gaze of the Kings of the Heights and subject to the uncanny incursions of the Tylwyth Teg. Into this chillingly enchanted land wander two fairy-tale innocents, Eloise and Simon. The former has led them there because she is pursuing communion with Mother Nature, of whose "benign concern" she's been assured by her New Age guru, Moonbird. But at Ty Coch it is the Old Age that holds sway – the *oldest* age, a time beyond the time of human computation and a nature anything but motherly. The watchers and their minions are creatures of chaos and old night, ancient as the hills and as indifferent as them to the well-being of the men and women who have strayed into their realm.

No doubt the overt fairy-tale apparatus of *Fairy Tale* – the Kings, the shape-shifting fairies, the changeling child – surprises and unsettles readers accustomed to the realism of the contemporary novel. *The Sin Eater* is a much more conventional novel by comparison; the weird entities of ancient Welsh legend and folk belief exist in that story without the same insistent autonomy that characterizes the rural Welsh supernatural beings of *Fairy Tale*. Psychology, in the earlier novel, seems more nearly to account for the out of the ordinary; in the later novel, as in several of Ellis's others over the years, the extraordinary is on an equal narrative footing with the quotidian. Immune to the quibbling of rationality, the extraordinary *is*. That this is so, fairy tale and fable have been telling mankind since we could tell ourselves stories. And Ellis's *Fairy Tale* thus takes its place in the company of those venerable tales.

A writer who has reviewed several of Alice Thomas Ellis's novels in the British press has praised her as the inventor of a genre all her own, "the supernatural comedy of manners."

I've touched on the supernatural elements of *Fairy Tale*, but what of the comedy? As in all of Ellis's work, the comedy of domestic manners is deft and deadly accurate and very, very funny. With that breathtaking economy which is such a hallmark of her art, Ellis captures the crepuscular London lives of Miriam and Clare, their long-standing, exasperated friendship and the frustrations and bitternesses of their respective entrances into confirmed middle-age. Their conversations sparkle with wit and cleverly phrased crankiness: Ellis's dialogue is always one of the great pleasures of her books.

I hope readers of *Fairy Tale, The Sin Eater,* and the many wonderful books in between, look forward as eagerly as I do to the next novel by Alice Thomas Ellis.

Thomas Meagher
Editorial Director, A COMMON READER

About The Author

ALICE THOMAS ELLIS is one of England's most widely admired writers. Her fiction includes *The Sin Eater* (1977), which received a Welsh Arts Council Award for a "book of exceptional merit"; *The 27th Kingdom* (1982), which was nominated for a Booker Prize; and *The Inn at the Edge of the World* (1990), which won the 1991 Writers' Guild Award for Best Fiction. Her most recent novel is *Fairy Tale* (1996). Alice Thomas Ellis has five children and lives in London and Wales.